THIRD TIME LUCKY.

BY

JOSIE METCALFE

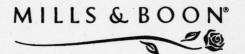

MILLS & BOON®

MILLS & BOON and MILLS & BOON with the Rose Device are registered trademarks of the publisher.

First published in Great Britain 1998
Large Print Edition 1998
Harlequin Mills & Boon Limited,
Eton House, 18-24 Paradise Road, Richmond, Surrey TW9 1SR

© Josie Metcalfe 1998

ISBN 0 263 15540 4

Set in Times by
Rowland Phototypesetting Limited

Printed and bound in Great Britain
by The ... *Iswich*

Her eyes took in her companion.

'Do you know,' Leo began in a musing voice, drawing her eyes up from their idle contemplation of the width of his shoulders to meet the striking golden fire of his own eyes, 'I think that's the first time you've ever really looked at me?'

Hannah was trapped by the intensity of his gaze, unable to look away from him in spite of the slow tide of heat which swept up her throat and into her cheeks.

'Don't. . .don't be silly,' she blustered shakily. 'We've been working together for more than a year.'

'Eighteen months,' he corrected her softly, almost as if he'd been keeping count. 'And the fact that we've been working together all that time doesn't mean that you've ever seen me as anything more than a colleague—until now.'

Josie Metcalfe lives in Cornwall now with her long-suffering husband, four children and two horses, but, as an army brat frequently on the move, books became the only friends who came with her wherever she went. Now that she writes them herself she is making new friends, and hates saying goodbye at the end of a book—but there are always more characters in her head clamouring for attention until she can't wait to tell their stories.

Recent titles by the same author:

SECOND CHANCE
FIRST THINGS FIRST
HEART SURGEON
VALENTINE'S HUSBAND
A WISH FOR CHRISTMAS

CHAPTER ONE

'OH, DAMN!' Hannah muttered with feeling as she clenched her fist tightly.

She'd only just found time to stop for a drink, and it wasn't until she'd reached out to switch on the kettle that she'd realised how badly her fingers were shaking.

It had been all right when she'd been busy. She hadn't had time to think of anything except the shocked and injured patients, firmly closing her mind to the fact that she knew so many of them.

Now, in the quiet of the staffroom, she was alone and the post-adrenaline reaction was setting in.

The explosion had happened so suddenly. . .

She snorted in disgust at the inane thought. . .as if an explosion could ever be anything other than sudden! But the fact that the blast had damaged the St Augustine's nurses' accommodation had been unbelievably shocking.

As the emergency team had swiftly donned

their protective clothing and grabbed their prepared kit, she'd found herself hoping that she
would be able to ignore the fact that she was
actually going to have to deal with her own
colleagues.

In the shattered remains of one corner of the
building there was the possibility that she could
find her friends trapped, maimed or even
dying. . .

No amount of experience could have prepared her for this eventuality, but she'd
managed to do as she always did if she wanted
to do her job efficiently—shut down the
personal emotions which would slow her reactions—and concentrated on following the other
members of the specially trained team into the
fray.

'Ah-h!' she breathed as she leaned her hips
back against the edge of the mock-onyx work
surface and took her first sip of the wickedly
strong brew, both hands wrapped firmly around
the sturdy mug—as if the hospital's notoriously
super-efficient heating had failed.

In spite of the warmth, she shivered, remembering the way Leo Stirling had followed the
firemen into the debris-strewn corridor, the
word DOCTOR glowing eerily across his back

under the emergency lighting and acting as a beacon for her to follow.

She'd dogged his footsteps as the rescue squad searched the building systematically and provided a supportive arm as each of the shocked inmates they located had been led out to the care of the paramedics to be ferried the short distance to the accident and emergency department.

It wasn't until she'd remembered following his long-legged stride up the stairs that the shaking had grown suddenly worse— remembered the way a heavy dread had settled in her chest when she'd been unable to shut the fear away any longer.

The gaping hole she'd seen from the outside of the building had seemed at first sight to have been right where her friend's room was, but she'd refused to admit to herself that anything could have happened to Laura.

They'd known each other for years—ever since they'd met during their training. If she'd lost Laura her best friend and a large part of her past would be gone for ever. . .

Oh, she realised that it was partly her own fault that she didn't have a wider circle of friends at St Augustine's, but she was too aware of the problems she could have if she allowed people to come too close—the explanations she would have to make. . .

She still shuddered when she remembered the embarrassment of a shopping trip with a group of her new colleagues shortly after she'd arrived to work at the hospital.

After an indulgent coffee-cake-and-chat session, where she'd been told all the inside stories about the rest of the staff on A and E, they had unexpectedly ended up in the evening-dress section of a large department store.

'Let's try on the wildest and most expensive things they've got,' one of her colleagues had suggested, and a third member of the group had eagerly agreed.

When Hannah had adamantly refused to join in it had cast a pall over the afternoon, and when the next outing they'd suggested had been a trip to the local swimming pool she'd realised that she wasn't ready for her problems to become common knowledge.

Sadly, she'd decided that, in spite of the fact that she'd always been a gregarious person, the only way she could cope now was to keep herself to herself.

The only person she'd felt she might be able

to confide in was Laura, and ever since her friend had joined her on the staff at St Augustine's she'd been trying to pluck up the courage to tell her what had happened in the time since they'd last worked together.

Now Laura was somewhere in the rubble of the room up ahead, and she might never have the chance to talk to her again.

'Hey! Wolff? What are you doing here?' she heard Leo demand through the buzz of her thoughts, and knew he was questioning his friend about his presence in a restricted area. Until it had been declared safe only emergency personnel were supposed to enter.

'I was already in,' a deep voice replied from inside the gaping horror of Laura's room. 'I was in the stairwell on my way up when it happened. What the hell caused it? It sounded like a bomb.'

'Gas main blew,' she heard Leo reply as he stepped into the room, his feet scrunching on shattered glass as he crouched down just out of her sight.

'How are you doing?' she heard him ask, and held her breath until she heard the reply.

'Apart from feeling as if I've been run over by a steamroller, I feel fine,' she heard Laura's familiar voice reply, and released her breath in one long sigh of relief.

That relief had made Hannah almost light-headed, and buoyed her up through the time-consuming routine mechanics of protecting her friend's neck, stretchering her out to the waiting ambulance and her own return to the department.

With the last few nurses needing careful stitching to repair the damage caused by flying glass, as well as the usual cross-section of 'routine' patients, Hannah barely had time to notice the way Wolff had shadowed her injured friend through her check-up in A and E.

At some stage it dawned on her that Laura wouldn't have a room to return to, and while she knew that the hospital management would have willingly found her accommodation she thought her own alternative would probably be the more attractive option—a chance to get right away for a few hours.

Perhaps she might even find the courage to talk to Laura and tell her about the events of the last two and a half years.

She waited the last few minutes to the end of her shift, but when she went to offer her friend a bed for the night in her own little flat it was to discover that Wolff was already helping her into his car.

She shrugged, initially piqued that Laura hadn't turned to her for help, but when the light fell across her friend's face and illuminated the expression in her gaze as she looked up at the darkly brooding doctor, leaning so solicitously towards her, she suddenly understood.

Ruthlessly ignoring the sharp twist of jealousy which pierced her again at the memory, Hannah buried her nose in the fragrant steam rising from her mug and took another sip.

She wasn't looking for a husband so why should she feel jealous of the fact that it looked as if Laura had found herself one. . .?

'Hey, beautiful, any more of that going?'

Hannah jumped with surprise when the cheerful voice accosted her from the other side of the room. She'd been so lost in her thoughts that she hadn't even heard Leo come into the room.

'I expect the kettle's still hot,' she murmured, glancing up warily as she stepped aside to allow him access.

'Hey, Hannah, how are you doing?' he demanded brightly, and she smiled wryly to herself. In his own inimitably charming way he'd obviously called her 'beautiful' without having any idea who she was.

She spared him a brief glance, then tightened her hands wrapped firmly round her own half-empty mug. There was no way she was going to risk letting him see how badly she was shaking—it would feel as if she were letting herself down in front of him. . .

They'd been working together for over eighteen months now, and she'd never come so close to letting her guard down in front of him—in front of anyone.

'That was a scary one,' Leo commented against the rising rumble of the kettle as he waited for the water to reheat.

Hannah kept quiet, hoping he would drop the subject, then groaned silently when he continued.

'Somehow it seemed much worse to know that it was our own we were going after, especially when we saw that great hole in the wall. It looked almost like the newsreel pictures of Beirut or. . .'

'Stop it!' Hannah said through clenched teeth, squeezing her eyes tightly against the pictures he was drawing in her mind. 'Please, just stop talking about it. . .' She couldn't go on and stood silently, shaking her head.

'Hannah?'

She heard the surprise in his questioning voice but refused to look at him, heat rising in her cheeks when she realised how badly she'd let herself down.

'Hey, Hannah, come on,' he coaxed, his voice strangely gentle as his hands descended on her shoulders.

Hannah froze.

'Leo. . .' she began as she tried to twist away from the contact, but he wasn't having any of it.

'You're shaking,' he murmured, as though he'd just made a startling discovery, and before she could formulate a single excuse he turned her towards himself and wrapped his arms around her, pulling her firmly against the solid warmth of his own broad chest.

'L-Leo,' she stammered breathlessly up at him, stunned by the sudden turn of events. 'Why. . .? What are you. . .?'

'Hush, woman. Can't you tell I'm giving you a hug?' he muttered in her ear as he brought his head down beside hers.

When Hannah felt the slight rasp of his emerging stubble against her cheek she drew in a startled breath, and with it an indefinable mixture of soap, laundry starch and male musk.

'But why. . .?' she began breathlessly.

'Shh. . .and put your arms round me,' he murmured just below her ear, and sent a sudden shiver skittering up her spine to lift the hairs on the back of her neck. 'I'm enjoying this, even if you aren't—a full-frontal cuddle with a beautiful woman is just what the doctor ordered at the end of a long hard day. . .'

At the sound of his husky voice she found herself complying mindlessly, and her arms wrapped themselves around the taut muscules of his lean waist, her hands flattening themselves against the stiff fabric of his white coat.

She drew in a deep shuddering breath at the overwhelming feeling of comfort that surrounded her and her heart produced an extra beat, almost like an exuberant skip in its normal rhythm. She was struck by a sudden lighthearted urge to giggle.

'Idiot!' she muttered as she tried to step backwards out of his encircling arms, feeling a little ridiculous now that her shaking was subsiding. 'There are any number of beautiful women in the hospital who would be willing to oblige you with a hug—Sexy Samantha, for instance,' she added in a burst of inspiration.

'Don't!' Leo protested with a shudder, his arms dropping away from her as if she'd just admitted to carrying a deadly plague. 'It's bad enough having to duck and run when I go past Obs and Gynae, without you taunting me about that barracuda!'

Hannah laughed at his terrified expression, not believing for a moment that he meant what he was saying—his reputation among the nurses was far too colourful for that!

Still, bringing up the voluptuous nurse's name had achieved what she'd hoped and there was now sufficient distance between the two of them to allow her to breathe more easily.

While he concentrated on making himself a mug of coffee Hannah took her own drink across to sit in one of the few high-backed chairs, curling her feet up under her for comfort.

For some time the two of them chatted easily about the events of the day, and Hannah was amazed how effective Leo's 'hug treatment' had been. There was hardly a trace of the awful shaking which had consumed her such a short time ago.

She allowed her mind to wander as her eyes took in the way her companion had sprawled himself across one of the small settees. She knew from standing beside him that he must be at least six feet tall but he looked much more than seven inches taller than she, with his long legs stretched out across the floor towards her own.

Her eyes travelled up the length of his dark trousers, the crease still sharp in spite of the long day, and she noticed the intricately braided belt around his waist.

Her attention was caught briefly by one of his collection of colourfully modern silk ties, bisecting his pale blue shirt, the knot of which hung low beneath the button he had loosened at the collar.

In spite of the fact that it was midwinter his skin still carried the remains of the colour he'd caught during the summer, and against the dark upholstery the tawny gold of his rumpled hair gave him the look of an indolent lion, apparently bonelessly relaxed but with the underlying feeling that he could leap into action at the slightest provocation.

'Do you know,' Leo began in a musing voice, drawing her eyes up from their idle contemplation of the width of his shoulders to meet the striking golden fire of his own eyes, 'I think that's the first time you've ever really looked at me?'

Hannah was trapped by the intensity of his gaze, unable to look away from him in spite of the slow tide of heat which swept up her throat and into her cheeks.

'Don't. . .don't be silly,' she blustered shakily. 'We've been working together for more than a year.'

'Eighteen months,' he corrected her softly, almost as if he'd been keeping count. 'And the fact that we've been working together all that time doesn't mean that you've ever seen me as anything more than a colleague—until now.'

Hannah drew in a shaky breath, realising with a deep quiver of unease that he was right.

She dragged the fingers of her free hand distractedly through her hair, feeling them catch on the tousled curls while she frantically cudgelled her brain to find the words to refute his assertion.

The sudden burst of sound as a group of colleagues trooped into the room broke the tension between them and she sighed with silent relief as he released her from the curious captivity of his eyes.

Strangely fearful that he might try to continue the conversation before she'd had a chance to marshal her thoughts, Hannah waited just long enough for Leo to begin talking to one of the group and then made her escape.

It had been a full day, with the added stress of the explosion in the nurses' home on top of everything else, and all she wanted to do was get back to her tiny flat as quickly as possible so that she could begin to unwind.

The last thing she wanted was a discussion with Leo about the fact that he was the first man she'd really looked at since Jon had changed his mind about marrying her. . .since he'd told her so bluntly that she was unlikely to find *any* man who would want to marry her.

'Wolff?' Hannah called as she hurried after him the following afternoon. She was on her way towards the staff canteen for her meal break and had just caught sight of him in the distance.

'Dr Bergen,' she called again, using the more formal mode of address when she realised how close they were getting to another group of staff. 'Can you wait a minute?'

'Hi, Hannah. What can I do for you?'

Wolff smiled as he turned and paced slowly

back towards her, waiting for her to catch up to him before he propped his hips on the narrow windowsill overlooking the winter-bare hospital grounds and folded his arms loosely across his chest.

'Sorry to hold you up,' Hannah began apologetically as she stopped in front of him.

The whole department had been only too aware of just how short-tempered he had been over the last couple of weeks and, although Hannah realised that she was probably the only one who had guessed that his bad mood had something to do with her friend, she didn't want to risk getting off on the wrong foot with him at the start of his shift.

'No problem.' He dismissed her apology breezily. 'I've got a couple of minutes.'

He smiled again and Hannah suddenly noticed what a change there had been in him over the last twenty-four hours. This wasn't the same man she'd worked with yesterday. *He* would have bitten her head off, rather than smile at her so easily.

'Oh. . . Well. . .' she floundered, completely put off her stride by the cheerful glow surrounding him. 'Actually, I just wanted to know how Laura is.'

'She's wonderful,' he said fervently, then cleared his throat when he realised what he'd just said. 'Sorry, that's not quite what you wanted to know, is it?'

'I don't know. Was it?' Hannah queried, bemused by the wash of colour riding high on his cheeks. What on earth had gone on between the two of them since she'd watched him helping her friend into his car last night?

'Laura's a bit battered and bruised from being trapped under the furniture but otherwise. . .' he shook his head in amazement '. . .she had a very lucky escape.'

'Do you know when she'll be back to work. . .and when the hospital is going to be finding her alternative accommodation? She's going to need some of her things in the meantime. Shall I bring her the basics after work?'

'I'll get her to give you a call about her things. If you *could* sort out a few essentials at the end of your shift I could take them back with me. I've told her she's taking a couple of days off—just until the stiffness goes away—but she won't be going back into staff accommodation.'

The last pronouncement was made in a very decisive tone of voice and Hannah's ears pricked up, especially when she saw him throw an almost furtive glance either way along the corridor. 'Actually, she's going to be moving in with me. . .permanently.'

'With you? But. . .' To say that Hannah was surprised was an understatement. She was almost speechless.

It hardly seemed more than a few hours ago that Laura had been telling her the details of the heart-breaking reasons for her decision to transfer to the A and E department at St Augustine's.

Although she'd known almost from the first that her friend was very attracted to the darkly handsome doctor, Laura hadn't known him very long and had given no hint about an ongoing relationship with Wolff.

Had the situation been precipitated by the traumatic events of last night? Was it gratitude for her deliverance from a life-threatening situation which had persuaded Laura to move in with. . .?

'I've asked her to marry me,' Wolff announced softly, his husky voice cutting across her scurrying thoughts as he met the concern in her eyes with his own icy blue gaze.

For the first time Hannah was allowed to see

the depth of the emotions he'd been keeping hidden, and suddenly she wasn't worried any more.

'We had a. . .a misunderstanding a couple of weeks ago and we've still got a few problems to sort out but I've told her I won't wait more than. . .'

'Married!' Hannah whispered, and a smile began to curve the corners of her mouth as his words sank in. 'That's wonderful! Oh, Wolff, I'm so happy for you both. . .!' She flung her arms around his shoulders and planted a noisily enthusiastic kiss on his cheek as he hugged her tightly, lifting her from her feet and swinging her around before he deposited her back on her feet again.

Hannah found herself beaming up at him, genuinely delighted that whatever had been making the two of them so unhappy for the last couple of weeks had apparently been resolved.

'Hey, Leo!' Wolff called over her shoulder and Hannah froze briefly, before wriggling herself hurriedly out of Wolff's friendly grasp and smoothing down her uniform as she turned to face the man striding towards them.

She'd hardly seen more than distant glimpses of him all day—almost as if he was avoiding her—and for her own peace of mind she needed to confront him to confirm the fact that her unexpected reaction towards him last night had been nothing more than her imagination working overtime.

After their strange interlude together she'd gone home to the quiet isolation of her tiny flat, bemused by mental images of his long-fingered hands wrapped around the steaming mug as he focused his tawny gaze on her.

She'd even imagined that there was a new heat in that gaze, a strange intensity in their deep golden colour which had made her quiver deep inside with a prickly awareness of her long-ignored femininity.

A sudden high-pitched bleeping made all three of them look towards the pager clipped at Wolff's waist. He pulled a face, but it was obvious to Hannah that nothing was going to be able to dim his happiness today.

'Got to go,' Wolff announced as he killed the noise. 'I'll see you later?' he reminded Hannah, referring to her offer to gather up some of Laura's belongings, and—at her nod—turned to his friend. 'I'll leave it to Hannah to tell you the good news, Leo,' he said with a beaming smile and a friendly clap on his shoulder, then he bestowed a totally uncharacteristic kiss on Hannah's cheek before he strode away.

'And what's put him in such a disgustingly cheerful mood?' Leo enquired as he shared a frown between Hannah and his friend's departing back. 'He's looked like a thunder-cloud for so long now that I was beginning to wonder if he'd forgotten how to smile.'

'Marriage,' Hannah explained with a broad smile as she began to lead the way towards the staff canteen. 'He proposed last night.'

'He did *what*?' Leo demanded, sounding utterly shocked as he came to a dead halt in the middle of the corridor, his hands clenched into tight fists at his sides.

To Hannah it almost seemed as if he'd gone pale at the very idea.

'Not everyone is as gun-shy as you are, Leo!' she teased, grinning up into his frozen face as she patted his sleeve consolingly. 'Some men actually decide they'd *like* to get married—like Nick Prince did, and now Wolff.'

'And you accepted?' he grated, his voice sounding almost rusty as it emerged from deep in his chest.

'*Me*?' Hannah squeaked in disbelief and

burst out laughing. 'Of course I didn't. He propos——'

She clapped a hand over her mouth and glanced around guiltily before she continued in a much quieter voice, remembering that it wasn't her place to spread the news around the hospital—no matter how accidentally.

'He didn't propose to *me*, you idiot!' she snarled as she dragged him to one side of the corridor, out of the way of a small group of curious junior nurses on their way out of the staff canteen. 'It's *Laura* he's in love with, Leo. He asked her to marry him when he took her to his house after the explosion.'

'Laura?' he repeated blankly. 'And she accepted?'

'Of course she did,' Hannah confirmed with a gleeful chuckle, wholeheartedly approving of the way things had worked out for her friend. 'Why wouldn't she? She's been in love with him almost since she clapped eyes on him with all those acres of bare muscles exposed by that exotic waistcoat at the Ball.'

'So. . .' She watched as Leo drew in a rib-cracking breath and considered the information. 'I suppose I can take the credit for engineering the meeting, can I?' he suggested, with the start of a smile lightening the golden colour of his eyes.

'Hey, it was my idea, too,' Hannah reminded him. 'Especially the part about swapping my ticket with Laura's. Otherwise *I'd* have been the one to go up on the stage with him, and he might have fallen for me instead.'

Leo muttered something under his breath, but before Hannah had a chance to ask him to repeat it his pager went off too and he made for the nearest phone.

'Drat,' she muttered as she helped herself to a tray and made her selection from the menu. She'd been looking forward to the chance of talking to him while they had their break.

Now that she thought about it she was quite enjoying the fact that once again the two of them were in the position of knowing privileged information about their colleagues, and she'd wanted the chance to gloat a little before the news became common knowledge.

At least she had one less worry on her mind, she thought as she drained her glass of orange juice at the end of the meal. The confrontation in the corridor had proved once and for all that she had no need to worry about Leo becoming interested in her—no need to worry that she might damage his ego by turning him down.

He'd obviously hardly noticed her in the eighteen months they'd been working together because he'd never have imagined for a minute that she'd accept a proposal of marriage from Wolff if he'd known anything about her.

And, she reminded herself as she approached A and E for the last part of her shift, she had no intention of entering into any sort of involvement with *any* man.

Especially not, she stressed to herself, a highly sought-after bachelor such as Leo Stirling, who had a ready smile for any female from six to sixty-six.

Furthermore—she continued her silent lecture—the situation was exactly the way she wanted it, and there was absolutely no reason why she should have felt a twinge of disappointment that he hadn't even noticed her, other than to sound aghast that his friend might have proposed to her.

Her inner debate continued for several hours as she worked beside Leo in the department.

She'd helped him to check over the young woman who had given birth to her first baby two weeks early while the ambulancemen transporting her had tried to battle their way around a choked temporary one-way system caused by yesterday's gas explosion.

'Here's a treat for sore eyes,' Ted Larrabee announced, beaming as he carried in his tiny blanket-swathed charge, Mike Wilson following closely behind with the surprised mother. 'Makes the whole job worthwhile.'

After a quick check-up Leo gave both mother and daughter a clean bill of health and they were transferred across to the maternity ward, leaving the A and E staff temporarily wreathed in smiles because they'd seen the beginning of a new life rather than more of the pain and ugliness they usually dealt with.

Unfortunately, the euphoria didn't last long.

The next patient brought in by the same ambulance crew meant a return to the grislier side of their job.

'Thirteen-year-old. Suicide attempt with paracetamol,' Ted detailed as he handed the belligerent youngster over.

Flushing the enormous number of tablets out of Sam's stomach was a task Hannah hated, and the whole situation was made so much worse when the distressed youngster cursed them for saving his life.

Hannah shared a horrified glance with Leo across the skinny body between them.

'I'll do it again,' the youngster rasped through a throat turned raw by the procedures he'd undergone, his eyes dull with resignation. 'If you send me back there I'll do it again, and next time I'll make certain that no one finds me in time.'

'Back where?' Hannah heard Leo ask as he waited for the next set of toxicity results to tell him how much of the drug had already been absorbed into the boy's system before it had caused the youngster to vomit and had given away his condition.

Although he wouldn't still be in A and E by then, she knew that it could take anything up to five days before they could tell how badly his liver function had been damaged.

In the meantime, there was Parvolex dripping down the IV line into his arm, mixed with copious quantities of five per cent glucose to keep up his fluid levels.

'Where?' Leo repeated, keeping his tone even. 'Send you where?'

'To the home,' Sam croaked despairingly,

and as he turned his head away from them Hannah caught sight of the single tear which slid across his temple and into his hair. 'I won't go back. I can't bear it any more. . .'

'Can't bear what?' Hannah prompted gently as she cleaned the evidence of the last hour's events from his face and wiped away the traces of the tear she was sure he'd never meant her to see.

'The polecat,' he muttered through gritted teeth, utter loathing in his voice. 'He's horrible and he smells and he does bad things to us kids. He hurts us.'

For the first time his determination and bravado had deserted him and his last three words had made him sound like the young child he was—only the stark fear and loneliness evident in his voice should never have been there.

Once again Hannah's eyes met Leo's and they shared silent communication about their suspicions.

'I'll just go and hurry those results up,' Leo announced quietly, and left Hannah beside their troubled patient to keep him company.

She knew that they both suspected that the lad had been the victim of some form of abuse in the home, and knew also that they were legally obliged to report their suspicions.

It would depend which paediatrician was on duty—Leo would be contacting them at that precise moment—but she knew that hospital policy would mean that the youngster would be admitted to one of the small side-wards so that he could be interviewed about his situation.

She could almost feel sorry for the misguided abuser, if it was, indeed, proved that the youngster had been injured in any way, because Ross MacFadden was the sort of consultant who believed absolutely in a child's right to happiness and love. She'd seen in the past how he went in to bat on behalf of his young charges without fear or favour, no matter how illustrious the abuser.

A member of staff in a position of trust at a children's home, whose activities had driven a young lad to attempt suicide, could expect no leniency.

'Right, Sam. I've got some good news and some bad news,' Leo announced when he returned, and Hannah watched the skinny shoulders go rigid as he waited to hear the worst.

'The bad news is that we're going to have to admit you to keep an eye on your blood until we know how many of the tablets have gone into your system. That means you could be here for several days.'

Hannah felt her eyes sting when she saw the relief flood through the youngster, his breath whistling out in a jagged stream. He'd obviously been terrified that, now that they'd emptied his stomach of its deadly burden, they were going to send him back into his nightmare. . .

'And the good news?' he croaked, finally meeting Leo's eyes.

'That you're going to be one of the lucky ones who gets a room all to yourself so you can choose the channel on the TV without an argument!'

'That'll make a change,' Sam commented wryly, the first hint of normal childish spirit lighting up his face. 'I might even get to hear the sound as well. . .'

CHAPTER TWO

By the time she came to the end of her shift Hannah was feeling quite cheerful in spite of the fact that the weather had deteriorated and there was rain lashing down in the darkness outside the windows.

Before she'd left the department to change out of her uniform word had filtered down from the ward that the lab results on Sam's baseline liver function and prothrombin time were looking good so far.

Her pleasure was tempered by the knowledge that the tests would have to be repeated every twelve hours to make certain that Sam wasn't going to deteriorate into liver failure, but she had a feeling that he was going to be one of the survivors.

His fear of returning to the home was a different matter, she thought with a touch of resentment as she scurried through the driving rain with a double load of belongings.

As far as *that* was concerned, she realised that it was unlikely that she would hear anything further about it unless Leo chose to speak to the paediatric consultant about the case and passed the information on to her. Even then, patient confidentiality meant that. . .

'No! You can't *do* this to me!' she wailed aloud in the chilly confines of her little car, smacking her hands on the steering-wheel in helpless frustration before she tried again to start it. 'Come on, you useless bucket of rust. Start!'

This time the engine barely whined at her and she gave up the attempt, staring out at the pouring rain in disgust. Her jacket was already sodden from her dash across the car park and her feet were soaking from the puddles she'd not seen in the dark.

Now the insides of the windows were rapidly misting up with the resulting condensation.

'What do I do next?' she muttered, agitated by her helplessness. She had no idea why the car wouldn't start, and there was no way she was going to stand about in the pouring rain while she tried to work it out.

'I can either run back inside the hospital to phone for the rescue service, and then hang around developing pneumonia while I wait for them to come, or I can pay for a taxi to take

me home now and sort out this rotten heap in
the morning.'

Hannah dropped her head back against the
restraint and sighed loudly when she realised
that either option meant that she was going to
have to brave the elements again.

She nearly jumped out of her skin when
something tapped sharply on the window right
beside her head.

For several seconds she sat there, with her
heart trying to pound its way out of her chest.
The windows were so opaque by now that all
she could see was a looming dark shape outside
the car, silhouetted against the yellow lights of
the car park. . .and in her hurry to get out of
the rain she'd completely forgotten her usual
safety precaution of locking herself in the car.

Sudden dread caught at her throat when she
remembered the way a colleague at her previous hospital had been stalked by an
ex-patient, and the level of her fear went up
like a rocket.

She couldn't even reach back towards the
lock to press the button down because she was
afraid the movement would be visible and
would tell whoever was outside that the car
was unlocked.

'Hannah?' called a male voice, the sound distorted into unrecognisability by the noise of the raindrops drumming on the car roof and splashing into the acres of puddles around it.

'Have you got a problem with your car?'

This time the voice sounded closer, and when she peered at the shadowy form outside the window she realised that he was now bending down so that he was level with the car window, his head just inches away from her own on the other side of the glass.

'Who. . .who is that?' she stammered in a shrill voice, her teeth chattering with a combination of fear and cold. She hardly dared to lift her hand to wipe the condensation away because while it would give her a clear view of the person outside it would also make her as visible and as vulnerable as a goldfish in a bowl.

'It's Leo, you idiot. Wipe the wretched window and look out before I drown out here!'

'Oh, thank God,' Hannah breathed, her first instinct being relief as she raised a shaky hand to swipe at the obscuring condensation.

Then anger roared through her.

'You're the idiot!' she shouted, her voice tinny in the confined space. 'You nearly scared me to death, tapping on the window like that!'

She glared out at him, getting her first good look at him.

Leo was even wetter than she was, his thick blond hair flattened against his head and so wet that it looked nearly as dark as Wolff's—a solitary strand curving down over his forehead to direct an annoying stream of raindrops down his nose.

'Has the car died, or do you just need a push?' he asked, apparently unmoved by her tirade, and she suddenly realised what a shrew she was being.

Knowing how temperamental the winder on her window was, Hannah opted to release the catch on the door and swung it open a scant inch so that they didn't have to shout at each other.

'I've got no idea what's the matter with it, Leo,' she said in exasperation. 'It was fine when I drove in this morning but it sounds as if the battery's too flat to turn the engine over now. Listen. . .' She tried the key again with the same miserable results.

'Did you leave anything switched on that could have drained it? The radio? The windscreen demister? The lights?'

Hannah had been shaking her head at each of his suggestions until he reached the last one.

'The lights?' she repeated, her hand going out to test the appropriate switch before she groaned. 'It was the lights. I had them on during a cloudburst when I set off from home this morning, but it must have cleared up by the time I got here so I forgot to turn them off.'

'Easily done,' Leo commented as he straightened up and grasped the top of her door. 'Now you need to decide what you want to do.'

Hannah peered up at him through the gap around the door while she tried to decide which of her options would be quickest, then realised that the poor man was getting wetter and wetter while she messed about.

'Look, Leo, there's no point in you hanging about drowning. I can either phone the rescue service or phone for a taxi and sort it out in the morning. You might as well go home and get dry.'

'Better than that,' he suggested. 'I could give you a lift home first. If we take the battery out of your car I could charge it up overnight so it will be ready to go back in tomorrow. Have you got a tool kit? It'll be bolted down and I'll need to take the leads off the terminals.'

'There's no reason why you should get filthy doing that—I can phone for the rescue service in the morning and—'

'You're wasting time, Hannah, and I'm getting wetter by the minute,' Leo butted in impatiently. 'Now, be a good girl—find the spanners and release the catch so I can get at the battery.'

He was standing beside the car with his fists on his hips, as immovable as a statue. His jacket collar had been turned up against the rain but, standing like that, the front edges had parted and his pale blue shirt was plastered over the breadth of his chest like an extra layer of skin.

Guilt at his sodden state made her give in without another word.

She scrabbled about in the glove compartment and came up with an adjustable pipe wrench.

'Will this do?' she offered meekly.

He pulled a wry face as he took it from her and disappeared around to the front of the car.

There were several scrapes and bangs behind the upraised bonnet of her car before he straightened up again with a familiar object in his hands.

'Right,' he said when he came round to her

window again. 'You can grab your stuff while I unlock my car. And don't forget to check that you've locked up,' he called over his shoulder as he strode away towards his own vehicle.

'There's not a lot of point locking the wretched thing—I don't think anyone's going to be desperate enough to steal a dead car,' she muttered under her breath as she dragged her eyes away from his long legs. She hadn't realised just how well muscled he was until she'd seen the way his wet trousers moulded around his thighs and along the lean length of his calves.

She shivered as she found herself doing as he'd said, gathering up her bag of belongings and the second carrier beside it before she remembered what it contained and where she had intended taking it.

'I've got a bag of things to drop off at Wolff's,' she announced apologetically as soon as she'd dived gratefully into the dry interior of Leo's car. 'They're some of Laura's clothes, rescued from her room.'

'No problem,' Leo said calmly, and her level of guilt rose another notch. He was absolutely soaking wet and it was all her fault. And now she was getting him to drive all over the place, running errands, when he needed to be going home and getting dry.

'Which bag?' he demanded. The words were startlingly loud in the heavy silence between them, and Hannah suddenly realised that the car was already parked behind Wolff's. She'd been so preoccupied that she hadn't even realised that they'd arrived.

She checked the contents of each and silently handed over the right bag, then watched while he loped swiftly up the path and rang the bell.

Light flared out briefly over him from the open door as he handed it over but he didn't linger—just a brief salute to his friend sufficing before he was on his way back to the car again.

He'd hardly closed the door before his whole body was convulsed by an enormous sneeze and her feelings of guilt escalated sharply.

'Would you mind if I stopped off at my place to grab a jumper?' he asked with a brief sideways glance towards her as he leant forward to flick the heater control up high.

For one brief second she longed to insist that he took her home first, but the lights from the dashboard were gleaming on the rivulets of water trickling down his face from his wet hair and she didn't have the heart.

'Of course I don't mind,' she agreed faintly and leant back in her seat again in a deliberate pretence of relaxation. It wouldn't matter so much if he did another detour—how long could it take him to get a dry jumper?

Hannah vaguely recognised the route they were taking, but it was on the other side of town from her own tiny flat.

She was quite surprised when the car drew up outside a building very similar to the one she lived in.

'This is where you live?' she queried. 'I would have thought you'd have something a bit bigger.'

'It's big enough for one,' he said in a quiet tone, which didn't invite any further comment.

As he pushed his door open to get out the wind caught it and flung it wide. In the space of the few seconds the door was open and the warm confines of the car were filled with a raw sample of the increased fury of the rising storm.

Suddenly it didn't feel quite so cosy any more and as she watched him walk around the front of the car she could see the way the wind was whipping his partially dried hair around his head in the few seconds before the rain plastered it down again, and she found herself wrapping her arms around her waist in an attempt to preserve her remaining heat.

'Come on,' Leo said shortly as he jerked open the passenger door. 'You'll freeze if you stay out here.'

'Oh, but. . .it's hardly worth me getting out just for you to grab a jumper,' she objected, strangely reluctant to go inside his flat.

She would be seeing the place where he lived, and even though they had been working together for eighteen months their relationship had been purely professional.

Somehow the thought of seeing where he relaxed and slept and entertained seemed far too intimate.

'No arguments,' he continued, brushing her objection aside as he reached for her elbow. 'Doctor's orders—I'll even throw in a cup of coffee to help thaw you out.'

Hannah grimaced, but once again did as she was told. She knew there was no point in debating the issue any further. If Leo had made up his mind. . .

'Ah, thank goodness for central heating!' he said gratefully as he unlocked his front door and they walked into the welcoming warmth.

He only paused long enough to drop the

catch behind them before he shrugged his way out of his jacket and reached for the hanger on the back of the door.

As Hannah watched, wide-eyed, he slid the knot of his tie down until it unravelled and then began to unbutton his shirt, his fingers struggling slightly with the stubborn wet fabric until it, too, was peeled away and wadded into a ball between long-fingered hands.

'I. . .' she croaked, then paused to clear her throat, suddenly concerned that he was going to continue to strip until he stood stark naked in front of her.

The only trouble was that she didn't know whether it was embarrassment at the idea of seeing her hospital colleague without his clothes or a secret excitement at the prospect of seeing even more of the virile perfection which had frozen her voice in her throat.

'Leo?' She tried again, and this time her voice worked. 'Shall I put the kettle on for coffee?'

'Wonderful idea,' he said with a grin as his hands reached automatically for the catch on his waistband. 'You'll find a coffee-maker in the corner, all ready to switch on, and there might be a packet of biscuits. . .'

His voice faded away behind her as she made her escape, aiming for the other door leading off the main room of his flat.

She flicked on the light switch in the kitchen and stood with her hands braced on the work surface, her head hanging forward as she mentally berated herself for her cowardice. If she'd stood her ground just a few seconds longer he'd have undone his trousers and she'd have seen. . .

'Here.'

His husky voice interrupted her heated musings and she whirled to face him with a scalding blush starting its way up her throat.

If he had any idea of the things she'd been imagining before he'd spoken he. . .

Her thoughts screeched to a halt when she saw him standing there, covered only by the towel wrapped around his hips.

'Here,' he repeated, holding out the twin to his own towel. 'You need to get out of that jacket and rub some of the wet out of your hair.'

Numbly she reached out for the bundle of soft towelling, her eyes darting helplessly from the width of his shoulders to the narrowness of his hips to the length of bare hair-sprinkled legs revealed by the towel before they returned to the amusement beginning to gleam in his strange golden eyes.

'You're covered in goose bumps,' she said, blurting out the first coherent words which popped into her mind.

After a second of startled silence Leo burst out laughing.

'Talk about keeping things in perspective!' he spluttered when he'd regained his breath. 'There I was thinking you were admiring my manly body!'

I was, I was, she declared silently while she fought to keep her eyes on the mock dismay filling his face. Even then his eyes were filled with good-natured mischief.

'You don't need me to stroke your ego by telling you that you're good-looking,' she said with a teasing smile of her own, proud of her steady voice. 'I'm probably the last nurse on the staff to see the proof, if the hospital grapevine is to be believed.'

For a second she thought she saw a shadow darken the light-hearted expression in his eyes, but it was gone so quickly that she couldn't be sure.

'You might be surprised,' he murmured

cryptically, and padded away on elegant bare feet, leaving her with the enticing image of tight male buttocks moving rhythmically under the precarious cover of his towel.

Hannah forbade herself to wish that the knot at his waist would magically unravel itself, horrified at the lascivious way her mind was working these days. Leo would be just as horrified if he knew what sort of fantasies were weaving their way through her head.

'Keep busy,' she muttered under her breath as she peeled her parka off and spread it open over the back of a chair in the vain hope that some of the wetness would have gone by the time she put it back on.

Not that she held out much hope—the rain had been falling so heavily that it had soaked right through her thin jumper.

She plucked at the damp fabric, horribly conscious of the way it was clinging to her and outlining the edge of her bra and hoping that was *all* it was revealing. . .

The coffee was made and Hannah was buried under the towel, briskly rubbing the worst of the wetness out of her short dark hair, when she felt a prickling sensation on the back of her neck.

Cautiously she peered out from the edge of the cloth and found Leo watching her as he leant against the frame of the kitchen door.

This time his lower half was covered in a disreputable pair of well-worn jeans, the seams rubbed so white that it was a wonder they still hung together and the waistband loose enough across the hollows of his belly to show her the path of the tawny hair that arrowed down from the width of his naked chest.

His towel was now draped around his neck, the hands holding each end curled into tight fists as his golden eyes spread fingers of fire over her body everywhere they touched.

Nervously Hannah cleared her throat, allowing her own towel to fall away from her head as she dragged her fingers through the tangled strands of her hair.

'Y-you wouldn't happen to have a comb I could borrow?' she asked huskily, consciously avoiding meeting the unexpected heat in his eyes. 'I—I left mine in your car.'

'As long as you don't mind sharing.'

One hand delved behind him into his hip pocket and came up with his wallet. As he padded silently towards her he flipped it open and slid out a narrow stainless-steel comb.

'Allow me,' he offered, beckoning with the comb.

'I can manage,' she said with a quick smile, holding her hand out for it. 'When I towel-dry my hair the ends can get in an awful tangle.'

Hannah started working her way through the knots and suddenly realised that Leo had returned to his position by the door and was still standing there watching her.

She froze, knowing that although it had nearly dried in the warmth of the room her thin jumper would be drawn tightly across her body by the position of her arms.

She glanced over at Leo and found that he had made the same discovery, his eyes making a very male examination of the visible curves and hollows revealed by her position.

Hurriedly, she lowered her arms, wrapping them around her ribs in a deliberately protective gesture.

'This isn't a very hygienic place to do this,' she commented as she tightened one hand around the comb until the teeth bit into her palm. 'Is it all right if I finish off in your bathroom?'

'No problem,' he said easily. 'You could have a shower, too, if you want. There's unlimited hot water and I can always find you some clothes to travel home in.'

'No!' she blurted, horrified by the idea of stripping off her clothes anywhere near him. It wasn't until she saw his frown that she realised how abrupt she'd been, and hurriedly began again.

'It's a lovely idea—especially in view of the fact that my hot water supply can be a bit erratic,' she said, smiling up at him while she frantically tried to find a cast-iron reason not to take him up on his offer, 'but I. . .I think I'd rather wait until I get back to my own flat then I can climb straight into bed afterwards.'

'As you like,' he agreed, his eyes travelling over her once more before he looked across towards the coffee. 'Did you find everything you needed?'

'The coffee's made but I hadn't looked for the milk yet.'

'I thought you took it black?' he said with a slight frown as he reached for the fridge door.

'During the day I do,' she agreed, unreasonably pleased that he'd noticed. 'But this late at night I usually adulterate it with milk so I can still get to sleep.'

She'd been watching the way his well-worn

jeans hugged his rear as he bent over to reach
for the bottle of milk, and had nearly missed the
official-looking notice painted in ornate black
letters on the white door.

'"Hangovers installed and serviced",' she
read out, and couldn't help laughing.

'That's a legacy of my student days,' Leo
said with an answering smile as he straightened
up with the familiar container in his hand and
nudged the door shut with one lean hip. 'I
shared a ghastly semi—'

'With Wolff?' Hannah butted in, remembering that the two of them had met during
their training.

'And two others.' He nodded as he poured
milk into her outstretched mug. 'We had a party
to celebrate passing some exam or other, and
one of our guests left us with an artistic
reminder of the event.'

'And you kept it?' Hannah blew on the
steaming brew and sipped at it gingerly to test
the temperature, before downing half of it in
one welcome draught.

'When we came to the end of our tenancy
the landlord took exception to the sentiments,
and we had to replace it or lose our deposit.

As it was still in working order I took it with me when we left.'

'And the fact that you've still got it doesn't have anything to do with sentiment at all?' Hannah teased light-heartedly, grateful that Leo's attention had been drawn away from her.

'Well, in mitigation, it *is* the only remaining evidence of my misspent youth,' he said with a grin, his eyes gleaming at her across the top of his own mug.

'You hope!' she shot back. 'We nurses get to hear all sorts of rumours about the things that go on during medical training—usually from the nurses who were invited to participate!'

'Not guilty!' he vowed with an innocent expression on his face, his free hand raised in surrender. 'I spent every night bent over my books, burning the midnight oil. . .!'

The mocking tone of Hannah's laughter told him just how much credence she gave that idea, but his words reminded her that she still had things to do before she could go to bed and she glanced up at the clock on the wall over his cooker before she hastily drained the last of her coffee.

'Speaking of midnight oil,' she began, turning back to face him. She was smiling as she met his eyes but when she saw the strangely hungry expression in his gaze suddenly it was as if there was no air left to breathe and the tension, which his nonsense had dispelled, returned full force to tighten all the muscles in her neck.

For the last few minutes they'd been talking and laughing in the same way they did in the department. Now all she could think about was the fact that the two of them were completely alone in his flat.

It wasn't a frightening thought—she couldn't imagine feeling physically threatened by him—but her emotions were a different matter entirely. . .

'Well, Leo, I'm on earlies tomorrow so I ought to be getting back,' she said, feeling the warmth rising in her cheeks when she heard how false her cheerful tone sounded.

She reached out to retrieve her parka but he got there before she could peel it off the back of the chair, one warm hand covering her own much cooler one.

For a moment he paused and she thought he was going to try to persuade her to stay, but then he took the heavy garment away from her.

'There's no point putting this back on or you'll be soaking wet again,' he pointed out. 'I'll lend you something of mine to keep you warm.'

'Oh, but. . .'

'Doctor's orders,' he continued, cutting across her objection as he led the way out of the kitchen. 'You can let me have it back tomorrow.' He threw her a strangely impersonal smile, as if he, too, was creating a distance between them.

She paused as he disappeared into his bedroom again and her foolish imagination ran riot as she listened to the sound of drawers being opened and closed.

Within minutes he returned and she wasn't certain whether she was pleased or disappointed that the upper half of his body had finally been hidden under a chunky-knit sweater.

'Here you are—this should keep you warm until we get you home.'

He handed her a deep blue sweatshirt, and when she put her hand out to take it she discovered that she was still clutching his comb tightly in her hand.

Awkwardly exchanging one of his belongings for another, she pulled the fleecy-lined garment over her head and breathed in a familiar scent. Was it his washing powder or fabric conditioner—or was it his own male essence transferred to the clothing by proximity?

Whatever it was, it made her feel strangely secure—as if she was once again being held in his arms instead of just being surrounded by his clothing.

'Ready?' he questioned when she slid her arms into the sleeves and found exactly how far they dangled past her fingertips.

'I would be if I could be certain that this jumper hadn't decided to swallow me up,' she quipped wryly as she tried to roll the cuffs back. The hem reached halfway down her thighs but, in the circumstances, that wasn't a problem— it would just make sure that there was less of her exposed for another soaking.

'Come on, then, little bit. You look like a child playing dress-up!'

'I'm not much more than six or seven inches shorter than you—less if I'm in high heels,' Hannah objected, stung by his indulgent tone.

'True,' he admitted as he came to stand in front of her and took over the fiddly task of rolling up the second sleeve. 'But your shoulders aren't as wide so the jumper droops down a lot further... Anyway, what's wrong with being petite? It can be very attractive to a man—brings out our protective instincts.'

She scowled up at him fiercely and he grinned back, tapping her on the nose with one finger.

'Of course,' he continued with a wicked gleam in his eyes, 'I wouldn't dare mention that with that expression on your face, and with your hair all tousled like that you make me think of a cat who went to sleep in a washing machine and didn't escape until she'd been fluff-dried.'

Before she had time to do more than draw in an indignant breath he'd swooped down and planted a swift kiss on her startled lips.

'Home,' he declared as she stood staring up at him with wide eyes, her lips still seared by a startling flash of heat at the unexpected contact.

A week later Hannah was still thinking about the lightning flash which had shot through her when Leo had brushed his lips over hers.

She still had no idea why he'd done it—there had been no warning that he was going to kiss her, and he hadn't even mentioned what he'd done either during her journey home or during their numerous meetings since.

She'd even begun to wonder if she'd imagined the whole thing. . .if it was some kind of mental aberration which proved that she was no more immune to charming bachelor play-boys than any other woman.

Unfortunately, every time she saw Leo around the department her heart would give that silly skip and she could feel her cheeks grow warmer. In contrast, he seemed to be completely oblivious to anything other than his work, while he effortlessly charmed every woman between six and sixty.

When she realised that she'd been allowing the event to dominate her thoughts for a whole week she decided it was time she gave herself a stern talking-to.

'Enough is enough,' she muttered aloud, squaring her shoulders with determination as she stood up after donning her boots at the end of her shift. 'There are more important things going on in my life than endlessly replaying a. . .a mere brush of the lips that the wretched man obviously forgot about as soon as he'd done it.'

In fact, one of the things which she had promised herself after Laura had been rescued was that she would finally take her courage in both hands and tell her about the events in her life since they parted company two years ago.

With the decision made, she set off to track Laura down and invite her for supper.

She hadn't cooked a meal for guests in all the time she'd been at St Augustine's, and it was about time she did.

CHAPTER THREE

'LAURA?' Hannah called as she saw her friend just disappearing around the corner.

'Yes. . .? Oh, it's you, Hannah,' Laura said with a big smile as she stuck her blonde head back around the corner. 'Come and join us. We've got time for a coffee before it's time to go.'

'Actually,' Hannah began as she caught up with her friend, 'I was wondering if you were busy this evening.'

She'd fallen into step with her smaller colleague as they continued towards the staff lounge and she couldn't help noticing an unmistakable eagerness in Laura's stride and an aura of happiness surrounding her—such a difference from the subdued person she'd been when she joined the staff at St Augustine's such a short time ago.

'This evening?' Laura queried with a slight frown as she pushed the door and held it open for Hannah.

'Yes. I was hoping to persuade you to come

round for a meal—it seems like ages since you started work here, and we still haven't had a chance to catch up on each others' lives.'

Laura looked a little puzzled.

'Oh, Hannah, I would love to but. . .didn't Wolff get a chance to speak to you alone this afternoon? We were hoping you would join *us* this evening. . .' She lowered her voice conspiratorially. 'It's a bit of a celebration, and it just wouldn't be right without *you* there.'

Hannah only had to look at the shining happiness in her friend's elfin face to guess what was going on. It was obvious that she wouldn't be returning to a room in the nurses' accommodation—Wolff had evidently made her a better offer. . .

'Oh, Laura,' she murmured with a delighted smile, keeping her voice low as she reached for her friend's hand and squeezed it. 'So this evening is by way of a celebration. I hardly need to ask if you're pleased with the situation?'

Laura beamed and nodded, her happiness spilling over like sunshine.

'In which case, I'd be delighted. Just tell me when and where.'

'At last,' a deep male voice grumbled before

Laura could answer, and Hannah saw the way the soft colour swept up her friend's cheeks when she saw Wolff waiting for her, his on-duty white coat and charcoal-coloured suit trousers long discarded in favour of a pair of smartly casual chinos.

For several seconds the two of them gazed silently into each others' eyes, their feelings so easily read that Hannah looked away, feeling almost like a voyeur.

'And another one bites the dust!' murmured a familiar husky voice in her ear, and she whirled around as if she'd been stung.

Leo.

She hadn't realised he was in the room, too.

'What do you mean?' she demanded, angry with herself when her voice emerged sounding as breathless as if she'd just run a marathon. Her heart had given that silly skip again, as though it were the first time she'd seen him in a week.

'Didn't Laura tell you?' he asked quietly, in deference to their friends' privacy and the scattering of colleagues around them. 'It's by way of a formal announcement.'

As she gazed up into his strange golden eyes Hannah was hit by a maelstrom of emotions.

First was the brief second of hurt that Laura had only agreed with her that the meal this evening was a celebration, rather than explaining what the occasion was, but this was followed by a renewed burst of pleasure that her friend had found such happiness.

Hannah felt the smile lingering on her face even as the familiar shadows crept out of their hiding places to taunt her that she was forever doomed to watch other people from the sidelines. Such happiness could never be hers. . .

'I take it you didn't know anything about it,' Leo said, his voice drawing her out of her less than happy thoughts.

'No. . . Apparently, Wolff was supposed to deliver the invitation but. . .' She shrugged in resignation.

Leo's eyes flicked down over her washed-to-death jeans, and she suddenly realised that he, too, was looking very smart—no well-worn jeans emphasising his masculinity tonight.

'Oh, Lord,' she breathed as she glanced across at the other couple and suddenly understood what was happening. 'It's not a pot luck meal—it's a fancy restaurant do and the rest of you are all done up to the nines.'

'Hardly,' he scoffed gently. 'But I think

you'll find that Laura's got a dress on under her coat, and I know Nick was taking Polly home to change—they're going to meet us there.'

Hannah hadn't realised that their boss and his new wife were coming, too, and when Leo mentioned the name of the venue she recognised it as one of the more exclusive little places on the outskirts of town—ideal for a once-in-a-lifetime special event like this.

Unfortunately all she knew about its location was that it was on the other side of town, and her heart sank when she glanced at her watch. There was no time for her to go back to her flat to change, then return to the hospital in time to follow the rest of them to the restaurant.

'In that case, I'm going to have to drop out,' she said with a wry smile and resignation in her tone. 'I'm not dressed for the occasion and there isn't time for me to go home to change, without making everyone else late.'

'There would be if I gave you a lift,' Leo pointed out, one hand already delving for his keys.

'What difference would that make?' she objected. 'You don't drive that much faster than I do, surely—unless that car of yours has hidden wings?'

'No, but I do know where we're going and I could take us both straight there when you've changed. . .' He left his words hanging in the silence between them, one dark tawny eyebrow raised questioningly while he waited for her to think.

'Laura would be upset if you didn't come,' he murmured persuasively as she was still undecided and with those words the decision was made.

Almost before she'd verbalised her agreement he'd grabbed Wolff's shoulder and, in a few low-voiced words, had told him what was happening.

'Let's go, then,' Leo declared briskly as he cupped her elbow in one warm palm and ushered her towards the door. 'They're just going to have a coffee and then they'll make their way to the restaurant. That gives us about twenty minutes to get you home and dressed.'

Hannah was having difficulty keeping up with his much longer legs as he strode along the corridor towards the closest exit to the car park or she might have found enough breath to challenge his choice of words.

As it was, the mental image he'd evoked of the two of them in her flat, getting her dressed together, had made her heart give its newly familiar skip, but it wasn't until the pictures in her head started to reverse the procedure—with his hands helping her to remove her clothing item by item instead—that she was able to regain grim control of her fantasies.

While Hannah fastened her seat belt she made certain to clamp down on her wayward imagination, and by the time she let herself into her flat she was able to be perfectly matter-of-fact about his presence there.

'Grab a cup of coffee, if you want. You could drink it in front of the television,' she offered as she made her way towards the bedroom. 'I shouldn't be much longer than ten minutes.'

'I'll believe that when I see it,' he scoffed, raising his voice so that it carried all the way through the flat. 'I've never yet met a woman who could get ready to go out in less than an hour.'

'In which case, you'd better keep your fingers crossed that I'm the exception to the rule or you're going to miss out on the first half of your meal,' she retorted as she rummaged speedily through her drawer for a clean set of underwear.

There was no problem in choosing what she was going to wear—there was only one item left in her wardrobe which was dressy enough for such an occasion. Everything else had been given away to a charity shop when she'd realised that she was never going to be able to wear them again. . .

'No time to think about that,' she muttered as climbed into the cubicle and had one of the shortest showers of her life.

In no time at all she had a towel wrapped around her dripping hair and was fastening her bra over skin which was still slightly damp.

Her legs weren't quite dry enough either and the tights she'd chosen for speed wouldn't slide up smoothly.

'Damn!' she muttered when she stuck her finger through them and made a huge hole. She knew she didn't have another pair so she'd have to go back out to the bedroom to replace them with stockings.

She wrapped her tatty old dressing gown around herself and opened the door, pausing a moment until she heard the sound of the television from the other room before she ventured out.

It wasn't that she thought Leo was so desperate for female company that he would resort to ambushing her in her own bedroom—it was just that she always felt so vulnerable when she came out of the bathroom without being fully clothed.

Her hands didn't stop shaking until she finally fastened the top of the silky midnight jersey outfit and smoothed it down over her hips. The wrap-over bodice was draped and pleated, cleverly disguising the fact that she was completely covered up to her throat—the whole design relying on subtlety to hint at the shape of the body it concealed.

Finally Hannah approached the mirror, rubbing her hair briskly for a moment before she ran a comb through it in the stream of hot air from her dryer. This was one time when she could be grateful for the fact that her natural curls would take care of themselves.

By the time she'd emphasised the deep blue of her eyes with a toning shadow her face didn't need any blusher, just a quick coat of her favourite lipstick and a last glance in the mirror at her hair.

With practised ease she scooped up her watch and bag with one hand and nudged her feet into slender-heeled shoes as she reached for the jacket hanging on the back of the door with the other.

'How was the coffee—nearly finished?' she asked as she walked into the other room, her attention on the watch strap she was trying to fasten one-handed. 'Have I taken too long?'

When there was no reply she glanced across the room, knowing that he would have found the only comfortable seat in the flat, and met Leo's intent gaze.

'What?' she demanded nervously, her hands growing still as his eyes travelled over her from head to foot. 'I'm sorry. . . Isn't it suitable?'

He blinked, almost as though he were waking up after a sleep and shook his head.

'Oh, it's suitable all right,' he confirmed, his voice sounding strangely husky. He cleared his throat and she felt a swift frisson of heat flicker over her skin at the unspoken pleasure in his eyes before she saw him drag them away to check his own watch. '*And* you made it inside the ten minutes!'

'Will you refuse to act as chauffeur if I dare to say I told you so?'

'Come on, woman,' he growled. 'It isn't nice to gloat.' He turned and led the way to her door, leaving Hannah to follow.

They arrived at the restaurant just as Nick Prince was helping Polly out of their car.

Something about the way he held her arm caught Hannah's eye and she paused thoughtfully as she waited for Leo to lock the car.

'What's the frown for?' Leo murmured as he reached her side. 'I thought you approved of the match.'

'Oh, I do,' Hannah agreed fervently, careful that her voice didn't carry as far as the other couple. 'If you remember, I did my best to push the two of them together.'

'Then why the frown?' he repeated, leaning back against the side of the car with his hands pushed deep into his pockets, apparently immune to the winter chill.

'It's nothing, really.' She dismissed his question but the intent expression in his eyes told her that he wasn't moving until he was satisfied.

'Well,' she capitulated, 'I was just watching the way Nick was hovering over Polly. He seems even more protective than usual, and it made me wonder. . .' She looked across, her eyes following the two of them as Nick ushered his wife into the restaurant, apparently so intent on her care that he was completely oblivious of his audience.

'Wonder?' Leo prompted.

'Whether *they've* got something. . .'

'Hey! You two!'

Wolff's call cut between them before she could voice her suspicions that there was more than one celebration going on tonight.

'Are you going to stand out there all night?' he demanded. 'There are people in here starving to death!'

Leo straightened up from his slouch against the car and waved.

'We're on our way,' he called back, and held out a hand to invite Hannah to precede him.

They were immediately surrounded by a welcoming warmth as they stepped inside the foyer and were escorted through to their table straight away.

'Here. . .let me,' Leo murmured as he helped her to removed her jacket and handed it to the hovering waiter.

His breath tickled the back of her neck as he bent over her to help her into her chair. It wasn't the first time in the last few days that she'd noticed this strange new awareness whenever he was near. She didn't need to look to know that he was standing close behind her, and the realisation set a tide of heat rising in her cheeks. She didn't know how she was going to manage to concentrate on her meal when he was sitting just inches away from her.

'Drinks, everyone?' Wolff offered.

'Just a minute,' Nick interrupted. 'In view of the occasion, I insist that this one's on me.'

'Certainly not,' Wolff retorted. 'Laura and I invited you all to help us celebrate. . .'

'And just beat us to the punch,' Nick continued mysteriously with a grin towards Polly. 'I suggest that we crack a large bottle of champagne.'

'That sounds promising—two colleagues arguing over who's going to pay for the bubbly—but I'm going to have to decline,' Leo said regretfully. 'It's orange juice for me.'

'Oh, Leo, no,' Laura commiserated. 'You're the one with the pager tonight?'

'John Preece is on duty, but if it gets too hairy. . .' Leo pulled a face and shrugged.

Hannah knew he didn't have to say any more. They all knew how easily a quiet night in A and E could turn into a bloodbath, with every available hand working flat out. All they could reasonably hope for was that Leo managed to get to the end of his meal undisturbed.

As expected, the food was wonderful—one perfect course following another—and as the six of them chatted easily among themselves Hannah found she was able to relax in spite of the the way Leo's arm tended to brush against hers.

As was usually the case with colleagues, the conversation began to veer towards work but Hannah wasn't surprised—with all of them working in the same department of the same hospital it was almost a forgone conclusion that it would.

'Ladies and gentleman,' Wolff said portentously when the dessert dishes had been replaced with liqueurs and coffee.

'Who?' mocked Leo, looking around as if wondering at Wolff's audience. 'You can't mean *us*!'

'Leo. . .!' Nick admonished with an attempt at a frown. 'Let the poor man have his time in the limelight.'

'I thought he'd already had that at the Autumn Ball,' Leo muttered in an aside to Hannah.

'And very nice he looked, too,' Hannah said with an answering grin. 'Beautiful tan, good body—and a lovely mover.'

'Hey!' Leo objected indignantly. 'You're supposed to be *my* date—you're not supposed to be ogling other men, even in retrospect!'

The burst of laughter from the other four told them that their conversation had been overheard and robbed Hannah of the chance to point out that she *wasn't* Leo's date. It had been purely coincidental that he'd been the one to bring her to the restaurant.

'If you two have finished wrangling?' Wolff asked pointedly, before he turned towards the green-eyed blonde beside him and captured her left hand in his. 'I would like you all to know that Laura has consented to marry me.'

While they applauded he slid an emerald and diamond ring onto her third finger, then raised her hand to his lips.

When Hannah saw the expression in her friend's eyes as she looked up at the darkly elegant man bending over her hand she felt the warning prickle of tears. She didn't think she'd ever seen her look so happy. . .

'And while you're all in the mood for celebration,' Nick added as he reached for Polly's hand and squeezed it, 'we'd like to tell you that we're expecting our first baby.'

'First. . .?' Polly squeaked, but her voice was drowned under the chorus of congratulations.

'*That's* what you were hinting at outside,' Leo muttered in a soft-voiced aside to Hannah. 'Was it just a lucky guess or had someone given you a hint?'

'I just noticed how protective he was being as he helped her out of the car—as if she was made of spun glass—and. . .' She shrugged.

'Well, I'm beginning to feel quite left out,' Leo complained to the group as a whole. 'You four are so happy it's almost abscene. There's Dr Prince grinning regally as he contemplates the start of a long line of princes and princesses, and there's Wolff smiling wolfishly as he volunteers to put his head in the trap. . .'

His awful puns on their names drew groans around the table, then he turned towards Hannah, his eyes gleaming at her like candle-light through expensive whisky.

'Well, Hannah, that just leaves the two of us,' he announced with one of his patented ladykiller smiles as he captured the hand closest to him. 'It seems to me that it would be a *sterling* idea if we got married as soon as possible.'

There were more groans and one exclamation of 'Leo! How unromantic!' from Laura, but Hannah was so startled by the unexpected declaration that she was grateful for the interruption, her mind going from blank surprise to utter turmoil in the blink of an eye.

Shock had adrenaline pouring into her system, altering her pulse and breathing in an instant as she stared up into his strangely intent expression.

He couldn't be serious, could he? It must be just one of his interminable jokes—the sort of thing which he could prolong for a whole shift if he found enough staff and patients willing to play along.

Deep inside, the vulnerable woman she'd once been relished the idea of his proposal, no matter how off-hand, but the eminently controlled, sensible woman she'd had to become knew she had to marshal a response. . .quickly.

'Oh, Leo,' she began, her voice far huskier than she would have liked, 'if only I'd realised earlier that you were feeling so left out I could have done something to make certain you felt wanted and needed. . .'

She'd been gazing into his eyes as she said the teasing words, pretending to simper up at him, until suddenly she realised that his pupils had dilated—almost as if he were becoming aroused—their strange colour darkening from whisky to brandy and their expression almost fierce.

'And if you'd realised?' he questioned, his voice deeper than ever. He was concentrating on her so intently that it was almost as if they were alone in the room. . .alone in the world. . . 'What would you have done to make sure I wasn't so lonely?'

Hannah blinked, wondering how she'd got herself into this situation—and how she was going to get herself out of it without making an utter fool of herself. What on earth had she been thinking of to tease him like that? Anyone would think she was flirting with him. . .that she had finally joined all the other females between six and sixty who kept trying to catch his interest.

In a blinding flash she had her answer, and she felt her lips curve into a smile.

'Easy,' she whispered with a hint of a pout as she dared to run the tip of one finger along the freshly shaven curve of his jaw. 'I'd have invited Sexy Samantha along to keep you company. . .'

'You teasing witch,' she heard him whisper under the hoots of laughter from the rest of the group.

'Oh, well done, Hannah,' cheered Wolff. 'You set him up beautifully for that one. Have you ever done any acting? That was definitely Oscar quality.'

Hannah found that she couldn't join in their amusement. She had seen the quick flash of challenge which replaced his pique at being bested, and wondered just how far Leo was likely to go if he did decide to reciprocate. Was she going to regret baiting him in front of their friends?

Nervous about travelling back with him, she waited until the general mêlée of retrieving coats before she tried to approach one of the couples for a lift, but it was almost as if Leo had read her mind.

'Here, Hannah,' he invited, holding her jacket open for her to slide her arms into the sleeves. 'It won't take long for the car to warm up but you might as well take as much warmth with you as you can.'

'Oh, but. . .' she began, glancing from the

wicked gleam in his eyes to the other couples performing the same ritual.

'Scared of me?' he taunted softly as he leant close to her ear, his warm breath aromatic with the scent of coffee. 'Scared enough to want to play gooseberry to either of those sets of lovebirds?'

He could hardly have chosen anything more likely to put the missing starch back into her spine.

'Of course not,' she hissed as she jerked her chin up a defensive notch. She knew as she said it that it was just the knee-jerk reaction he had been looking for, and the fact was confirmed when she saw the swift gleam of triumph lighten his eyes.

'Well, then, beautiful, let's go home to bed,' he invited with a wicked grin, his voice just loud enough for his words to carry to the rest of the group.

The expressions on their faces ranged from shock and surprise to speculation and concern, but Leo didn't give her a chance to explain that they would be returning to their own separate beds.

There was just time for a swift farewell before he was ushering her rapidly towards the door and out into the darkness, his silent efficiency leaving her almost breathless.

She hesitated about berating him for his deliberate *double entendre* in front of their friends, realising that it wasn't safe to argue while he was trying to concentrate on his driving, but he apparently didn't have the same scruples.

'Your place or mine?' he questioned slyly once they were on the road, the car's heater efficiently dispelling the wintry chill from her feet.

Hannah drew in a slow silent breath as she chose her words, tempted to let fly. How dared he presume that just because she had accepted a lift in his car they would be spending. . .

At the last second sanity prevailed and she realised that outraged reaction was probably exactly what he wanted. She knew from working with him that he was a past master at stirring people up.

A second slower breath gave her time to rein in her anger and consider a different course.

'Whichever is more convenient for you,' she said calmly as she unknotted her fingers and folded them neatly one over the other on her lap. 'If you'd rather not drive the extra distance

I can always walk. It's not that far.'

There was silence for a moment, as if she'd startled him, then she heard a soft chuckle and she dared a glance at him just in time to see the wry expression on his face in the intermittent glow of the streetlights.

'You know, Hannah, if you worked at it you could be very bad for my ego,' he murmured.

'Really?' she said, hardly daring to believe that he was already prepared to joke about the situation. She'd known other men who wouldn't have been able to accept such a calm dismissal without pushing the point.

'Yes. Really,' he confirmed, obviously having to try very hard to sound disgruntled as he fought a grin. 'I use my very best chat-up lines on you, and what do you do. . .swoon with delight. . .scream with excitement. . .accept with alacrity. . .? No such luck. *You* remain perfectly unaffected and suggest walking home!'

Perfectly unaffected? Hardly, she thought as she mentally replayed the images which had assailed her when he'd first said he was taking her home to bed. She had a good enough imagination to know that the naked, golden-skinned body she'd imagined in that bed was a fair approximation of Leo's, but if he ever found out that she'd so readily imagined herself in the bed with him she'd never hear the end of it.

'Your very best chat-up line?' she scoffed, latching onto something. . .anything. . .which would take her mind away from the image of a stark naked Leo sprawled across her bed like an indolent lion. 'Your place or mine?' she repeated and forced a chuckle.

'You don't mean to tell me you've heard that line before?' he demanded in horrified tones, and the chuckle turned into shared laughter.

Within minutes he was drawing up outside her flat, and she was startled to realise how much she was regretting the fact that their time together was over.

'Well, thank you for the lift,' she mumbled as she searched feverishly for the doorhandle. The sooner she could shut herself inside her flat the sooner her brain could start functioning normally again. 'There's no need for you to get out. . .'

Too late. She was talking to his knees as he straightened up out of the car and shut his door.

Hannah huffed out an exasperated sigh as she swung her feet out to the pavement, then resigned herself to making polite conversation for a few minutes while Leo did the gentlemanly thing and escorted her to her door.

As he took her elbow she admitted secretly that she actually enjoyed the feeling of security his hand gave her. She wouldn't dare to admit it among her more feminist friends but she regretted the fact that so many of the old-fashioned courtesies between men and women were dying out.

'I enjoyed myself this evening,' Leo said suddenly as they reached the step in front of the door, the angle of the building sheltering them from the chilly wind.

'You sound surprised,' Hannah said with a smile as she turned to face him. 'Weren't you expecting to?'

'Yes and no.' His expression was wry as he went on to explain, his breath forming a frosty halo around them. 'The three of us—Nick, Wolff and I—have been friends for a long time, and with the demands of our careers we've sometimes gone months or even years without getting together.'

'Rather like Laura and I?' Hannah suggested.

'Probably.' He nodded, the light over the door striking gleams of gold off his hair and highlighting the clean masculine lines of his face. 'But, even so, when we *do* see each other it's as if we can carry on the conversation exactly where we left off.'

'Laura and I are like that,' she confirmed with a laugh. 'I was a bit concerned when she said she was coming to St Augustine's. I was afraid that in the two years since we last worked together we might have grown too far apart to pick up the threads or that new friendships, such as mine with Polly, might have taken over.'

'*That's* what I was afraid of tonight—that with the new bonds the other two had formed with Polly and Laura the bonds between the three of us would have been broken.'

'And instead?' Hannah prompted, interested to hear his thoughts in spite of the fact that the cold was gradually creeping through the warmth of her jacket.

'Instead, it's as if the bonds have somehow stretched to accommodate the changes in the relationship. . .as if Polly and Laura have slotted into niches that were ready and waiting for them. . .'

He paused when she couldn't hide her shivering any more, his eyes moving swiftly over her as if he had forgotten how lightly she was dressed for the time of year.

'Oh, Hannah, I'm sorry,' he apologised, wrapping a penitent arm around her shoulders, as though to share his own heat with her. 'Here I am prattling on about nothing while you're freezing.'

The warmth of his body seared her from shoulder to thigh as her questing fingers found the key in the bottom of her bag and, in spite of their insidious trembling, she managed to unlock the door on her first try.

'I wouldn't have listened if I wasn't interested,' she pointed out as she stepped into the warmth of the minuscule hallway and then, on an impulse, held the door open to invite him to follow her inside.

'Coffee?' she offered, a different sort of shivering beginning inside her when she realised exactly how long it had been since she'd invited a man into her home.

Leo's face creased into his trademark ladykiller smile as he followed her inside, but before he could speak there was a familiar high-pitched bleep.

Hannah's heart sank with swift disappointment but the expression of disgust on Leo's face as he batted the thing into silence made her chuckle aloud.

'The phone's through here,' she offered as she led the way into her sitting room and switched on the lamp on the side-table.

'Thanks,' Leo said, his voice preoccupied as he concentrated on tapping out the familiar number.

The conversation was brief and to the point, and Hannah soon realised that there had been an horrendous crash of some sort on the motorway.

'How many trapped?' she heard him demand, and she could visualise the sort of scene which would have met the rescue services—she'd seen it often enough at first hand since she'd become a member of the mobile emergency team.

'I'm sorry, Hannah, but I've got to run,' he said as soon as he broke the connection. 'Can I take you up on the offer of coffee another time?'

'I expect so,' she said absently, her concentration more on the last words of his conversation on the phone. 'Did I hear you say they were having difficulty contacting one of the team members?'

Leo nodded and threw the name of one of Hannah's nursing colleagues over his shoulder as he made his way back towards the door.

'She's been off with flu. They thought she was ready to return but she's not answering so it looks as if the team is going to have to be short-handed tonight.'

'Not necessarily,' Hannah said decisively as she kicked off her strappy high heels and stripped off her best jacket and flung it haphazardly towards the arm of a chair. 'If you can give me ten seconds to grab my anorak and a pair of trainers I can take her place.'

CHAPTER FOUR

'SOMETIMES I don't know which I hate most about an English winter—when it rains or when it doesn't rain,' Hannah said with a heavy sigh as she crumpled up another length of used disposable sheeting.

'Why's that?' Tina Wadland glanced up from her own task, her gloved hands continuing to wipe down blood-spattered surfaces.

'Well, when it rains some stupid idiot will always forget how slippery wet roads are and travel far too fast and too close to the car in front. Then something goes wrong and everyone has to brake suddenly, and we end up with this. . .' She gestured with the bowl of blood-soaked swabs before she disposed of it.

'So?' Tina's hands had slowed into a repetitive circular movement. 'Surely it's better when it doesn't rain?'

'Ah, but at this time of year when it doesn't rain they're so delighted that they forget how low the temperature can drop at night and forget about black ice so that when they have to brake suddenly. . .'

'A clear case of heads you lose, tails you lose,' a familiar husky voice broke in, and Hannah whirled to face Leo, her eyes racing over him with guilty pleasure.

He was leaning lazily against the work surface closest to the doors, his ankles crossed and his white coat pulled back by the hands thrust casually into his trouser pockets, his pale blue shirt adorned by yet another of his collection of brightly patterned silk ties. This one was an abstract symphony of terracotta and turquoise in the midst of the hospital monochrome.

He hardly looked as if he'd missed hours of sleep last night, she thought as her eyes finally reached his face, peeved that he looked as alert as ever while she was feeling distinctly ragged.

Mind you, she admitted silently, that could be because he'd gone straight to sleep when he finally got to bed while she'd tossed and turned, endlessly reliving the events of the evening like a tape loop in a projector. It had been after three o'clock the last time she'd glared at the glowing numbers on her alarm clock.

'Any news on those people last night?'

Hannah questioned when she managed to find her tongue.

'We haven't lost anyone else,' he confirmed, his smile dimming as he, too, remembered the horrific events which had been the culmination of the previous night.

He hadn't bothered arguing with her spontaneous offer of assistance—a nod and a briefly muttered 'see you in the car' had been enough to indicate his acceptance.

Within a minute they'd been on their way to the hospital, the journey virtually silent as they'd geared their minds up for the task ahead.

'A minibus went out of control on the motorway,' was the greeting they'd received when they'd arrived. It hadn't been until Hannah had seen eyebrows going up that she'd remembered that the two of them had still been dressed for their celebration meal, but everyone had been too preoccupied to comment. Tomorrow would be different. . .

'Fire and police on the way, and we've called in an additional mobile medical team from St Mary's as they're not the designated hospital. Estimates of fifteen casualties, several trapped.'

The briefing went on as Hannah stepped behind a convenient stack of shelving to don her protective clothing. There was no time for niceties such as changing in a cloakroom— people could be dying.

She was still pulling on her reflective tabard over her green arctic anorak as she slid into the back of the vehicle, the layers of tracksuit and waterproof boiler-suit making her feel terribly clumsy after the soft clinginess of the dress she'd just removed.

There was a quick burst of static on the radio before they left the shelter of the hospital building, then they were on their way, speeding through the darkness.

'Any more information yet?' Leo demanded, leaning forward against his seat belt.

'They think the driver of the minibus either fell asleep at the wheel or had a heart attack. The vehicle swerved across the road and, of course, everyone else started trying to get out of the way. . .'

Hannah saw him shrug. He didn't need to say any more.

'Mayhem,' Leo muttered, confirming her thoughts, and slumped back against the seat again.

For the first time Hannah saw the fourth member of the team sitting on his other side.

'Hi, Nia,' she murmured when she saw the familiar outline of the other nurse.

Nia Samea smiled, her teeth very white against her dark olive skin in the subdued light.

'Wish we didn't have to meet like this so often,' she commented in her softly lilting voice. 'But at least this time we've not having to rescue our friends.'

'We do seem to have had more than our share of call-outs recently,' Hannah agreed.

'One of the hazards of working in a front-line hospital with all the latest bells and whistles at our disposal,' Leo added wryly, then sat up straighter as the brightness of the emergency floodlights up ahead told him they had arrived.

'Oh, my. . .' breathed Nia when she caught her first glimpse of the chaos which awaited them. 'There are bodies everywhere. . .'

The vehicle detoured on the direction of one of the policemen at the scene, and they came to a halt at the command centre beside the generator which was supporting one of the towering floodlights, illuminating the carnage.

'How far have you got? Where do you want us first?' Leo demanded as soon as his feet hit the littered tarmac.

'We've set up a casualty collecting station,'

confirmed the senior policeman who was obviously in control at the command centre. 'Two paramedics from the ambulance service have started triage, but there are too many victims. Can your team split up. . .one half to the collecting station and the other to those still trapped? Obviously, in these sort of temperatures the faster we can get them shipped back to St Augustine's the better—we don't want to add hypothermia to their problems.'

Leo turned to their group to direct them.

'John, will you and Nia take the collecting station and sort the wheat from the chaff? Hannah, come with me.'

He set off at a brisk jog, his bag carried as easily as if it were just an extension of his arm, the fluorescent bands on his uniform gleaming eerily in the harsh light.

Several members of the fire service were clustered around the minibus, the jaws of life already being positioned to scissor their way through the front doors to provide access to the injured trapped inside.

'Doc. . .over here!' called a voice, and Leo veered around the back of the vehicle towards the fluorescent striped beckoning arm, with Hannah close on his heels. 'Can you check these two before we begin?'

The expression on his face let them know that he wasn't hopeful for the outcome of the venture, but that obviously wasn't affecting the efficient way he did his job.

The impact of the crash had come primarily at one side of the front of the vehicle, and the diagonal forces as another car had slammed into the back had twisted it so badly that none of the doors could be opened.

Leo reached in through the shattered windscreen, the reflective bands on his own protective clothing almost blinding at close quarters.

Over his shoulder Hannah could see him trying to find a pulse in the patient's neck. She was only a young woman, Hannah thought as she waited alertly in case Leo needed her to pass something. From what she could see, the patient was probably much the same age as herself but one side of her head and face had been badly injured, probably on impact with the side of the window frame, and her long blonde hair had an ominously large dark patch right down one side.

Leo's gloved hand was bright with blood when he withdrew it, shaking his head.

'No hurry for that one,' he muttered succinctly as he stepped back to look for the best way to clamber over the wreckage towards the person in the driver's seat.

'Nor that one,' the fire officer added bluntly, grabbing Leo's elbow to save him the journey as he gave his crew the signal to continue. 'He was partially decapitated on impact, but there are others trapped inside.'

He indicated the route they had started clearing through the side panel of the minibus, their machinery opening it up like some monstrous tin-opener.

While he waited for the space to be widened sufficiently Leo strode towards the car which had rammed into the back of the minibus. It looked as if the engine must have ended up on the driver's lap. . .

'Has this one been checked?' he called as he bent down to peer inside.

'No good,' the fire officer called back over the noise surrounding them. 'Broken neck—probably instantaneous on impact.'

Hannah watched Leo straighten up, his expression grim as he strode back to the bus, arriving just in time for a large panel to be peeled back.

'Can we get some more light in this side?' he called as he was cleared to approach and leaned inside.

'God, what a mess,' Hannah whispered when she saw the state of the interior. 'Where do we start?'

Leo's mouth tightened as he silently held his bag out towards her and climbed gingerly between the ragged edges of the hole. She stepped closer so that when one hand reached out she was ready with the handle within reach.

'Is there room for me?' she asked, peering into the jumble of seats and upholstery, people and belongings she could see tangled together.

'Give me just a minute. . .' There was a pause of a few seconds before several armfuls of extraneous baggage came sailing out into the road. 'OK, Hannah, you can come in now, but watch yourself—there's a lot of glass and sharp metal. . .'

One of the fire crew took charge of her bag but it wasn't until she tried to climb up into the bus herself that she realised how much easier Leo's long legs had made it for him.

Another fireman took pity on her predicament and solved it instantly by lifting her up bodily so that she could thread her feet into the hole.

'Thanks,' she muttered with a brief smile as she twisted back to retrieve her bag.

She turned to focus on the interior of the minibus and the outside world ceased to matter.

Several of the passengers were obviously unconscious, if not worse, but some were coherent.

'Please, help me,' whispered one crumpled figure as she raised a hand in supplication. 'I hurt so much. I—I think my leg's broken.'

Hannah crouched beside her, carefully manoeuvring between the severed upright struts of one of the damaged seats.

'Where does it hurt?' she asked gently as she began her examination, her fingers automatically reaching to feel for the woman's pulse.

In the end she didn't need the young woman to tell her where the injury was—the jagged edges of the shattered bone sticking up through the blood coating her thigh told their own story.

'Leo,' Hannah called, knowing just how quickly such an injury could cause a patient to go into shock from the amount of blood lost into the thigh itself. With an exit wound as large as this, the loss could even cause death. 'I've got a compound fracture of a femur here.'

She heard Leo relay the message outside and, as she reassured the increasingly drowsy young woman that help was on its way, she swiftly found a vein in the patient's hand.

By the time the ambulancemen arrived to work out how they were going to stabilise the leg and extricate the patient she was ready to attach the bag of fluids to the needle she had taped in position.

It took nearly ten minutes to help the poor woman out, her cries of pain muffled by the Entonox mask as they finally lifted her out through the gaping hole.

Two of the women were unconscious but, apart from large knots on their heads, they appeared to be uninjured.

'Sorry to take so long getting them out of your way but we have to put a neck collar on each of them and get them on boards, just in case there's any spinal damage,' one of the younger ambulanceman explained, totally unnecessarily.

Hannah didn't comment. She knew that safety first was the best maxim if they weren't to cause further damage to their victims in the process of getting them out. It would be dreadful if one of the passengers had survived the crash, only to be paralysed by an injury to the spinal cord in the rush to get her out of the vehicle.

She was just about to work her way forward to the next victim when a sound in the corner behind her drew her attention.

'Has anyone mentioned that they were carrying pets on board?' she asked as she warily made her way towards the noise—a strange mixture of panting and growling.

'It's all right,' she said soothingly as she got closer to the shadows, worried that an injured animal might lunge out at her in panic. 'I'm not going to hurt you,' she continued in as reassuring a tone as she could manage while she peered at what appeared to be a large mound of clothing.

'Please. . . Help me. . .' whispered a hoarse voice, the words broken up by ragged breathing. 'It's. . . My baby's coming. . . It's too early. . .'

Hannah's blood ran cold when she heard the terror in the voice emerging from the shadows, and she scrambled forward as fast as the obstructions would allow.

'Woman in labour,' she called over her shoulder as she cleared a space for herself at the woman's side, and heard Leo swear succinctly.

'How is she? Any injuries?' he demanded across the shambles separating them. 'I've got my hands full for a minute. . .'

'Were you hurt in the crash?' she asked the labouring woman as her moans began to escalate. Hannah's fingers automatically reached for the hand she could see in the dimness, seeking a pulse.

'My arm. . .!' yelped her patient. 'It hurts like. . .like hell. . .'

Now Hannah could see that the poor woman was cradling one arm with the other.

'Is that the only place you're hurt?' she asked, frustrated by the fact that the lights didn't quite reach this corner. 'What about your head?'

'No, that's. . . Oh, God. . . Here comes. . .another one. . .'

Hannah had begun to stroke the dark hair back from the woman's forehead while she asked for details, such as her patient's name and age, but when she realised that the contractions were almost continuous she knew there was no time to waste on bedside manners.

She'd just turned to shout for the ambulancemen to bring the supplies she'd need to
help Sara Pethick bring her baby into the world
when the young woman caught her wrist in a
grip of steel.

'It's coming,' she panted suddenly. 'I can
feel it. . .down there. . . I want to push. . .'

'No!' Hannah ordered fiercely. 'Don't
push. . .not yet!'

'Oh, but. . . I've *got* to. . .!'

'Pant! Please, you must pant until I can check
that the baby's all right.'

'But it's ready to come. . .' Sara wailed as
she tossed her head restlessly from side to side.
'I can feel it!'

'Just give me a minute to check that everything's ready,' Hannah pleaded. 'You've still
got your underwear on and. . .and you don't
want to hurt the baby, do you?'

It was half plea, half emotional blackmail,
but it seemed to work.

'Quick! I need some more light over here,'
Hannah snapped over her shoulder as she
helped her patient out of her underwear,
moving as quickly as she could. 'And an oxygen cylinder and a sterile obstetric kit.'

She longed to ask questions about the prematurity of the infant, but she didn't dare distract the mother-to-be from her panting. Not until this contraction faded and she was able to make her examination. . .

As someone angled a powerful torch towards her the level of light increased in her niche behind the back row of seats, and she suddenly saw what was happening.

'Oh, God,' she breathed, then closed her lips firmly, hoping the young woman hadn't heard the horror in her voice.

'Leo,' she called over the cacophony surrounding the vehicle, fighting to keep her voice calm as her discovery forced her to rearrange her plan of campaign. 'She's got a prolapsed umbilical cord.'

She mentally crossed her fingers that the words would be meaningless to her patient, but she and Leo both knew that the young woman's unborn baby was now in great danger.

She heard the urgency in Leo's voice as he handed over the care of his present patient to another pair of willing hands, then heard his voice getting nearer.

'I'm bringing the oxygen and the upholstery from one of the seats to elevate her hips.'

Hannah had to shuffle across on her knees

to allow him to wedge himself in the limited space beside her, immeasurably relieved to have him working so closely with her.

'What's happening?' the young woman demanded hoarsely as the urgency to push died away for a moment. 'Is something the matter with my baby?'

'Your baby's fine,' Leo said soothingly as he signalled silently for Hannah to help him lift the young woman's hips. 'We just need to put a cushion under you. . .'

The upholstery from one of the broken seats was slid into position as easily as if they'd practised the manoeuvre many times, tilting Sara's hips to help relieve the pressure on the protruding cord.

A gloved hand passed Hannah the sterile obstetric kit over her shoulder and she tore it open immediately, careful to touch only the outside of the package until she'd had time to clean her hands.

'Here,' a disembodied voice said over her shoulder, and she turned to see a bottle of povidone-iodine scrub solution apparently suspended in mid-air.

'Thanks,' Hannah muttered as she stripped off her contaminated gloves and held her hands out under the liquid, grateful that whoever the administrator was had recognised the need for speed.

As soon as her hands were clean she leaned away to reach into the open kit for a fresh pair of gloves, allowing Leo to take his turn with the scrub solution.

She turned back to their patient just as the next contraction began building.

'Pant!' she reminded Sara when she groaned, pleased to see that Leo had been able to position the Entonox mask and hoping that it would be enough to dull the urge to push. 'Keep panting!'

'I'm going to have to catheterise,' Leo murmured. 'If I can get half a litre of saline into her bladder and clamp the catheter shut then the full bladder will alter the pressure between the head and the pelvis and help to stop the blood supply to the placenta being cut off.'

Hannah nodded her comprehension, carefully keeping her hands out of the way. She knew that when the cord arrived ahead of the baby the danger was that it would become trapped between Sara's pelvis and the baby's head. If that happened the baby would be asphyxiated, its brain dying when its supply of oxygenated blood was cut off.

'Are you ready for a bad case of cramp?' he muttered under his breath.

'Ready.' She nodded again and bent forward to position her fingers against the baby's emerging head and push it gently back up into the vagina until the cord was free, the thick dark loop once more pulsating strongly.

As she settled her fingers around the tiny head she tried to find the most comfortable position—she knew that Leo hadn't been joking about the probability of cramp.

As she watched him swiftly catheterise the woman, carefully timing the task between contractions, Hannah knew that, no matter how uncomfortable she got, if they wanted to save the baby's life she was going to have to hold the position of her hand against the baby's head until they managed to get the young woman out of the minibus and into the ambulance which would transport her to hospital.

Only when there was someone else there to maintain the pressure against the baby's head would she be able to relinquish her position.

Leo leaned around her to cover the exposed cord with a sterile dressing moistened with saline, and draped an apparently endless supply of towels and blankets around the shivering woman to preserve her body heat.

When Hannah heard him draw in a breath she knew he wasn't relishing having to explain to the young woman exactly what was going on and, while she maintained her own position, she watched as he gently broke the news about the baby's problem and what they were doing about it.

It took an agonising half-hour for the combined teams of firemen and ambulancemen to extricate Sara from the minibus, time that Hannah spent quietly talking to the increasingly agitated young woman, encouraging her to stay calm for her baby's sake.

Leo had received an urgent call elsewhere to administer morphine and make a decision about a possible emergency amputation and had been forced to remove himself from the scene, but the time he had spent gently explaining the complication seemed to have allayed Sara's most pressing fears for the time being.

Hannah was amazed at Sara's resilience when she heard later that the young woman had actually been able to crack a joke with the ambulanceman who'd taken over her intimate task for the duration of the journey to hospital.

As Hannah ruefully massaged her hand she

watched the ambulance speed on its way towards St Augustine's, grateful that Sara had been far too involved in her own predicament to think about the fate of her fellow passengers.

After her baby was safely delivered would be soon enough for that.

In the meantime. . . She flexed her fingers one last time before she retrieved her bag and set to work again.

It was another two hours before the last ambulance left for the hospital, this one travelling without flashing blue lights. There was no need for haste with its final sad burden—the bodies of those who had lost their lives.

'Let's get back to base,' Leo murmured as he wrapped a comradely arm around her shoulders and gave her a brief squeeze. 'You must be shattered.'

'Well,' Hannah conceded as she slid gratefully into the comforting upholstery of their rapid response vehicle and leaned back, 'all I can say is it certainly isn't dull, spending time with you.'

'All the girls say that,' Leo quipped smugly. 'I'm well known to be a fun person to date.'

'Are you two going out together?' Nia demanded from her corner, instantly interested enough in the gossip potential of what she'd heard to rouse herself from an exhausted slump.

'No. . .!'

'Yes.'

They answered simultaneously, but Hannah couldn't believe what he'd said. Didn't he realise that this wasn't the sort of thing to joke about if he didn't want it to spread through the hospital like wildfire?

She glared at him.

'No, we *aren't* going out together,' she said, firmly contradicting him.

'So where were we earlier this evening?' he demanded mildly, both eyebrows raised in interrogation and a fugitive smile playing at the corners of his mouth.

'At a restaurant with Nick and Polly, and Laura and Wolff,' Hannah said impatiently. 'But—'

'And who took you there and brought you home?' he continued inexorably, obviously playing to the gallery as both John and their driver were now listening too.

'*You* did,' she confirmed. 'But—'

'I rest my case,' he interrupted, not allowing her to continue.

He finally allowed his wicked grin to show.

'I took you out to a meal in a restaurant with a group of friends, then brought you home again. Now, doesn't that sound as if she's going out with me?' he demanded, turning to appeal to Nia.

Much as she would have liked to set the story straight, Hannah was too tired to argue and had to be satisfied with turning her back on the wretched man and his far too interested audience until she could get away from them.

Even when they arrived back at the hospital, it didn't prove easy. She'd been thanking her lucky stars that her own car was still parked in the staff car park and she wouldn't need to rely on Leo for a lift, but he was still waiting for her when she emerged from the cloakroom, dressed once more in her 'dining-out' finery.

'Hannah. There you are.' The familiar husky voice startled her. She'd been hoping that he would be otherwise occupied until she could make her escape.

'Leo.' She smiled wanly up at him, her breath hitching in her throat when he captured her elbow and began to escort her towards the exit closest to the car park.

'You don't need to walk me to my car— there are plenty of lights for safety. . .'

'I just thought you'd like an update on Sara,' he said mildly, totally ignoring her objection as he ushered her out into the frigid darkness.

'How is she?' Hannah demanded, totally sidetracked by his change of topic.

'She had a little girl and she says she's going to call her Hannah in your honour.'

'Oh, Leo. . .!' she breathed, emotional tears flooding her eyes. 'Is she all right. . .are they *both* all right?'

'Little Hannah is apparently raising the roof and couldn't be better, and Sara's getting plastered!'

'Oh, I'm so glad. She was so brave. She went through everything without a murmur, in spite of her broken arm.'

'And it couldn't possibly have anything to do with the calmness and courage of the nurse who held more than her hand throughout!' Leo teased as he turned her to face him, cradling her cheeks in his hands and gently wiping a single escaping tear away with his thumb.

'It was a team effort,' she objected, in spite of the warmth his praise sent flooding through her. 'The whole team was fantastic—we didn't lose anyone else at the scene of the accident, and. . .'

She bit her lip, suddenly aware that she was babbling. Had the warmth of his hands short-circuited her brain?

Leo was smiling down at her, his teeth very white in the artificial light and his eyes seeming to glitter as he looked down into her face.

Hannah shivered as a strange tension began to grow between them.

'Well, it's certainly been an eventful evening,' he said, his voice almost distracted as his eyes travelled from her eyes to her mouth and back again. 'Perhaps we should try it again some time. . .?'

Hannah gazed up at him, not quite certain what he was suggesting, but before she could ask his head had swooped down and his lips brushed over hers.

CHAPTER FIVE

THE memory of that fleeting kiss had haunted the hours of darkness.

One moment Hannah was reliving the soft warmth of his mouth on hers and revelling in the accompanying surge of excitement, and the next she was chastising herself for overreacting to what was little more than a friendly salute.

But why had he done it? She'd been working with him for nearly two years now and he'd never shown any interest in her before. Was he at a loose end with no new partner in sight? Had that kiss been part of his infamous seduction technique—the one that was rumoured to turn knees to jelly in every department in the hospital?

She snorted in silent disgust at her own nonsense.

As if someone as downright handsome and charismatic as Leo was likely to restrain himself to such a milk-and-water effort. It was only because it had been so long since she'd received *any* kisses that she was reacting this way.

Anyway, there was no point in getting herself in a state over it—it wasn't as if there would be any more kisses to worry about. Jonathan had let her know in no uncertain terms that no man would ever be interested in her unless he was desperate, and Leo certainly wasn't desperate. He could take his pick of the most beautiful. . .

'Hey! Hannah! Are you asleep on your feet?'

It was Tina Wadland's voice which called her back to the present, and she blinked owlishly as she looked around.

What was she doing? What was she supposed to be doing?

'Sister MacDonald was looking for you,' Tina continued once she knew she'd got Hannah's attention. 'She wanted to know if you'd come back from your break so she can send the next lot off.'

'I'm coming,' Hannah confirmed as she swung herself round on the stool in the corner of the tiny kitchenette and slid her feet down to the ground. She grimaced when she saw the state of her cold coffee and tipped it down the sink. 'Just give me two minutes in the bathroom and I'll be firing on all cylinders.'

'Thank God for that,' Tina commented as she began to walk away. 'The world and his wife seem to have decided to pay us a visit today, and there's a new woman on duty in Reception who seems to think it's her right and duty to make everything as difficult as possible.'

'As if life isn't difficult enough,' Hannah muttered to Tina an hour later when she'd ushered out yet another patient who had spent the entire time he was being treated complaining about the receptionist's obstructive attitude. 'Enough is enough.'

'What are you going to do?' Tina called as Hannah began to stride away down the corridor.

'I'm going to bring in the big guns,' Hannah said, and threw a grin over her shoulder before she elaborated. 'I'm going to set Big Mac on her!'

Hannah entered the main reception area and looked around for the familiar spry figure of the diminutive senior sister, knowing that she was just as likely to be seen out here as closeted in her office.

The doors slid open silently and a tall man

strode in, with a child of about eight cradled in his arms. Father and son bore such a striking resemblance to each other that there was no mistaking the relationship, and they were both looking pale and worried.

It wasn't until he gently deposited the boy on the floor by the receptionist's desk that she saw that one hand was wrapped in a blood-soaked towel.

'My son's put his hand through a glass door,' the man said, one arm comfortingly around his child's shoulders, regardless of the fact that his immaculate suit was in imminent danger of getting blood-stained.

'Name?' demanded the receptionist, with barely a glance in his direction as she began tapping self-importantly on the computer keyboard.

'Ben Thomas.'

'Is that Ben or Benjamin?' she asked disapprovingly, her hands suspended over the keys like petrified spiders.

'Benedict,' he supplied patiently.

Click, tap, tap, tap. . .

'Address?'

Once again he supplied the information in a calm voice but Hannah could see that it was only a façade he was maintaining for his son's sake and she set off quickly towards him.

'Date of birth?' Click, tap, tap. . .

The next question coincided with the limits of the man's patience. Hannah had seen his agitation rising as he watched the spreading pool of blood dripping from his son's elbow, his free hand clenching spasmodically in his frustration.

'For God's sake, woman!' he exploded just as Hannah reached his side. 'He's damaged an artery and he's bleeding heavily. If this nonsense goes on much longer I'll be able to give you his date of death as well!'

For the first time the officious woman actually looked up from her keyboard.

'Well. . .!'

'If you'd like to follow me, sir,' Hannah suggested quietly, cutting across the woman's outrage.

'I can't let him go *yet*, Sister. He hasn't finished filling in the details. . .' she began pompously.

Much as she would have liked to have given the woman a piece of her mind, Hannah ignored the bleatings going on behind her and led the way swiftly towards the trauma room. It was enough for her that she'd seen Celia MacDonald bearing down on the reception desk with fire and brimstone in her eyes.

Later she would make certain that Sister had heard both sides of the story, but for now her job was to take care of one brave but very frightened young lad.

Once his father had settled him on the high bed he retreated to the other side and held his son's free hand.

Hannah carefully unwound the once-white towel and found that the gash on the youngster's arm was every bit as bad as she'd imagined, running diagonally almost the length of his forearm.

The towel was almost saturated with blood and the poor child was beginning suffer shock.

'How did you do this?' she asked, partly for information and partly to take the child's mind off what she was doing.

'Ant—my little brother, Anthony—pinched my car and I was trying to catch him. He ran inside the house and pushed the door shut behind him to try and stop me.'

'And you put your hand up to stop it shutting?' she questioned as she quickly wrapped a sterile dressing over the gaping wound.

'Yes, and the glass broke. . .' He hissed with pain as she applied pressure to slow down the bleeding, and Hannah apologised.

She caught sight of the expression on his father's face when he saw his child's discomfort and swiftly enlisted his help, showing him how to take over the job of maintaining pressure over the damaged artery. As she'd expected, he was only too pleased to feel that he was doing something to help.

'If you can hold on there for a second I'm just going to grab the doctor from next door,' Hannah said, and quickly suited her actions to her words, her hands held out of contact with the doors as she used her hip and shoulder to exit the room.

'Leo,' she called softly as she pushed open the swing doors to the room next door, easily recognising his burnished hair and broad-shouldered physique as he bent over his own patient.

'I need you next door for a moment,' she continued, sternly dragging her eyes away from her unaccustomed appreciation of his physique. 'I've got a young lad next door who's put his arm through a pane of glass. It looks as if he's nicked the radial artery and he's bleeding pretty badly. I've got him head down because he's already in borderline shock.'

Leo's head turned towards her, his eyes tiger bright over his disposable mask.

'Nerves? Tendons?' he rapped out over his shoulder as he turned back towards the still figure in front of him.

'Probably,' Hannah said, correctly interpreting his shorthand as a demand to know about the involvement of other structures in the boy's arm.

'Get a saline IV up and running straight away and send blood samples up to the lab for cross-matching, ready for Theatre. I'll be with you in two minutes.'

Hannah ducked out through the doors again and turned immediately into the next set.

'Right, Ben,' she said. 'I need some information from you.' Out of the corner of her eye she saw his father begin to bristle, but she surreptitiously winked at him and watched him subside into watchfulness.

'Tell me, do you ever watch any hospital programmes on television?'

'And vet programmes.' The bright-eyed youngster nodded, obviously determined to fight the side-effects of his accident. 'Dad says

I'm the bloodthirsty one in the family.'

'So you know a bit about the equipment we use?' she asked as she collected the items she needed. 'Like masks and gloves and needles and transfusions?'

'Yes,' he nodded, the slightly wary look which entered his eyes telling her that he was intelligent enough to have worked out just where this conversation was going.

'So, if I was to talk about an IV you would know what I meant?'

'It's a needle with a tube on it for putting something into someone,' he said. 'Is that what you're going to have to do to me?'

There was a slight quiver in his voice and Hannah longed to give him a reassuring hug. He might be trying to be very grown up and brave, but he was still only a boy. . .

'You've been losing blood ever since you cut your arm, and we need to put some liquid back into you so you won't dry out and blow away.'

'What sort of liquid? Blood? Will it. . .hurt?'

Hannah couldn't help smiling and was glad she was wearing a mask so he didn't think she was laughing at him. It was touching the way his keen inquisitiveness had given way in the end to natural fear.

'You'll probably be having some blood put in later, but at the moment I'll be putting some saline in—that's water with a tiny bit of salt in it. It might hurt just for a second when the needle goes in,' she admitted honestly, 'but when we put the saline solution in you won't feel a thing.'

'Oh.' He gazed up at her for a moment before he looked back at his father for support and drew in a shaky breath. 'OK!' he said, and held his little paw out to her.

'Good boy,' Hannah praised, then concentrated on getting the needle in as quickly and as painlessly as possible.

'How's that?' she said when she straightened up. 'Did I do it as well as they do on TV?'

'Yes, but. . .you said I was losing blood so you had to put s-saline in—' he hesitated over the unfamiliar word '—but then you took some of my blood *out* and squirted it in a tube.'

'That's right. And now I'm going to write your name on the label and send it up to the labs. They're going to test it so they can match it up in case you do need to have some blood put in.'

'There's a chance that he might be AB nega- tive,' his father interrupted, 'in which case you can have some from me—I'm a regular donor.'

'How long ago did you last donate?' Leo asked as he walked into the conversation and grabbed a fresh pair of gloves.

'Nearly six months ago—the mobile unit comes round twice a year and they're due soon.'

While he'd been talking Leo had gestured for him to release his hold on the dressing over his son's arm. After he'd done so Leo gently peeled it back to have a look at the damage.

'Well, there's some good news and some bad news,' he said when he straightened up after a thorough examination, one hand sup- porting the injured arm as he applied pressure over the vital area. 'The good news is that the cut is so clean and sharp that there's a good chance that it will mend just as cleanly.'

'And the bad news?' Mr Thomas prompted, his face still very grey.

'The bad news is that he's going to have to go up to Theatre for this to be stitched up.'

'Why?' Ben demanded shakily. His eyes had been going from one adult to the other while the conversation went on across him. 'Can't *you* do it?'

'It will need the special microscopes they have up in the operating theatre so they can see clearly enough to join everything up in the right order,' Leo explained with a patient smile. 'You've cut one of the arteries in your arm and you also caught some of the tendons so we want to make absolutely sure that we don't miss anything.'

Mr Thomas was looking as if he would rather go through the whole thing himself than sit by and watch his son suffering, but the youngster seemed to have accepted the situation remarkably quickly.

'Will I be able to see the microscope?' Ben demanded as Hannah took over and rewrapped his arm and then, at his request, let his father resume responsibility for maintaining pressure over the wound.

Meanwhile, Leo's long-legged stride had taken him over to the phone and he was waiting to be connected with the surgeon who would do the job.

'That's all arranged, then, Ben,' he announced when he turned back to them. 'As soon as you're ready to go up the surgeon will

give you a quick look at his operating microscope, and then you'll be put to sleep so that
he can use it on you.'

'Really?' He might be pale and injured, but
there was nothing wrong with his enthusiasm.

'Thank you, Doctor,' Mr Thomas said with
a tired smile as the tension began to show.
'You've been very kind.'

'It's the least I can do for Ben. After all, he
made two bad mistakes today.'

'Two?' Ben questioned looking from one
adult to another with a frown.

'Yes. The first one was in putting your hand
through the glass in the first place, and the
second one was in putting the *wrong* hand
through it—even after the operation you won't
have to miss any school!'

Ben's groan was nearly as loud as his
father's chuckles.

With a quick salute and a grin Leo left the
room, and it wasn't long before Ben was on
his way up to Theatre, his trepidation lightened
by the prospect of a glimpse at hospital tech-
nology.

Hannah set to putting the room to rights.

Last time she'd looked there had been a

queue of people waiting—some more patiently
than others—and all wanting attention.

By the time she came to the end of her shift
she felt as if she'd attended to half of the population of the town. They were at the beginning
of the annual flu season but this year it seemed
to have started early, with every other person
complaining of a cough, a high temperature or
a headache.

In between there had been splinters to
remove from a large naked bottom, the owner
of which refused to detail how it had happened,
and stitches to be removed from under a child's
chin, collected as the result of an argument with
a school playground.

There had also been four assorted lacera-
tions, three broken limbs, two suspicious chest
pains, 'and a partridge in a pear tree,' Hannah
muttered as she reached for the small pile of
letters in the 'N' section of the internal mail
system and sorted through for any with her
name.

'Just one,' she sighed as she peeled the flap
open. She quickly scanned the computer gener-
ated appointment letter and her heart sank like
a stone.

Had time really passed so quickly? Was it time for her next check-up already? At least they hadn't given her too long to think about it.

She stuffed the letter back into the envelope and shoved it roughly into the pocket of her parka.

'Bad news?'

Hannah jumped and whirled to face the owner of the voice. She hadn't even realised that Leo had entered the room, let alone that he'd been standing right behind her.

'No. . .just an appointment I'd forgotten about,' she said with a calmness which belied the trembling inside.

That had been too close, she thought. He could have seen the letter over her shoulder and then her secret would have been revealed. He certainly wouldn't be smiling at her if he *had* seen what the letter was about. . .

'If it's something you want to talk about,' he offered softly, and she suddenly realised that her thoughts must have been mirrored on her face, 'I've got broad shoulders, if you need to use one. . .?'

She cast her eyes over the width of his chest and slid them upwards. He certainly did have broad shoulders, and they looked as if they would be infinitely comforting to burrow against if everything went wrong again.

If she'd had someone like Leo to rely on last time when her whole world had fallen apart everything would have been so different. As it was, she'd been totally alone and had been forced to turn inside herself and draw on her own strengths.

That was when her self-sufficiency had been born, and she hadn't regretted it for a moment until now. . .

'Thank you,' she murmured quietly, bending forward to pick up her bag to avoid meeting the keenly analytical look which had replaced the puzzlement in his whisky-coloured eyes. 'I'll bear that in mind.'

Suddenly the last couple of days caught up with her and she couldn't wait to reach her own tiny haven and lock the rest of the world out for a few hours.

'See you tomorrow,' she said with a quick dismissive smile, and hurried out of the room.

As she drove through the freezing darkness she laughed bitterly to herself.

Leo would never know how lucky he was that she hadn't taken him up on his offer. Knowing what a devil-may-care sort of character he was, he would probably have been horrified if she *had* told him about her problems.

The most frightening thing was that, for the first time, she had actually been tempted to tell someone all about it, just for the relief.

She hadn't even told Laura yet, and they'd been friends for years, so why on earth she should think about confiding in someone like Leo. . .?

Perhaps it would be better if she erected the barriers again and kept the world at its customary distance. She would hate to ruin the wonderful working relationship she'd built up with her colleagues, and she knew that if they found out about her past then everything would change.

Her preoccupation with her impending appointment made it all too easy for Hannah to keep everyone at arm's length—even Laura.

It had felt as if something inside her was tearing apart when she saw the hurt in her friend's eyes when she repeatedly turned down invitations to join her to make up a four or a six with Nick and Polly or Wolff and Laura.

Unfortunately she knew who the other

member of the group would be, and she'd already seen his expression harden when she'd refused his every invitation—even a cup of coffee when their breaks coincided.

Oh, she'd made certain that no one could complain about her attitude to her work—she was still just as dedicated and hard-working, and she still joined in the jokes and laughter within the department—it wasn't in her nature to mope around with a long face.

The trouble was that she couldn't help her attraction towards Leo. It seemed that once her feminine awareness of him had awoken it refused to go back to sleep, and working with him only made her realise what a genuinely nice person he was.

Many was the time over the next few weeks that she sat alone in her tiny flat and chuckled at the memory of some bit of nonsense he'd perpetrated during her shift. . .some trick he'd played on another member of staff or a joke he'd told a frightened patient to try to help them relax.

She'd laughed longest at the running battle he seemed to have, trying to stay out of Sexy Samantha's predatory clutches—his detours into sluices, behind curtains and into linen cupboards descending into farce as he begged the A and E staff to save him from her.

His behaviour seemed very out of character for one of the most charismatic bachelors on the staff and, in spite of her determination to keep out of his way, Hannah found herself aiding and abetting his avoidance tactics with growing glee.

It was two days before Christmas before she realised that her wish had come true. In the discomfort of the aftermath of his kiss and all it could represent she had longed for a return to the relaxed relationship that the two of them had always enjoyed when they worked together.

As she reported for the start of her shift she glanced at the board to see which other members of the team were sharing the duty with her, and was pleased to see Leo's name without a qualm—in fact, she was actually looking forward to spending the time with him.

She smiled at the prospect of the seasonal silliness he was bound to bring with him and refused to admit that she still harboured a niggling regret that she hadn't been able to risk seeing where that fleeting awareness might have led the two of them.

The Leo who reported for duty was anything
but the embodiment of life and energy she had
been expecting. When he walked through the
doors his face was almost grey and his stunning
golden eyes were dull and red-rimmed.

'Heavy date last night?' taunted one of the
charge nurses with an all-men-together leer on
his way through, and blinked when his words
were totally ignored.

'Late night, Leo?' He tried again, obviously
expecting to see the trademark grin and cheeky
reply.

'Something like that,' Leo replied sombrely
and walked away.

Hannah filed his response away and determined to find out what was wrong. She hoped
that Leo saw her as a friend now and, as far
as she was concerned, friends cared about each
other and Leo wasn't happy.

After a morning of his strange mood, Celia
MacDonald was obviously concerned, too, and
readily agreed to release Hannah for her break
as soon as she saw Leo disappearing in the
direction of the staff lounge.

'Here,' Hannah murmured a few minutes
later as she held out a steaming mug full of
black coffee.

He hadn't even looked up when she followed him into the room and set about filling the kettle and switching it on.

He'd gone across to the window and perched one hip on the corner of the sill so that he could gaze out at the dull wintry scene outside.

'What. . .? Oh, thanks, Hannah,' he murmured absently, wrapping both hands around the thick pottery mug as though he were freezing, before he returned his gaze to the depressing prospect of soggy brown grass and bare trees.

'Is. . .is there anything wrong?' she ventured, her heart going out to him. He seemed as if he had turned in on himself in the few hours since she'd last seen him.

He'd been his usual cheerful self yesterday. . .

The last time she'd seen him, when she'd been on her way out of the department at the end of her shift, he'd been teasing one of the junior nurses about what presents she wanted from Father Christmas.

What had happened in the meantime?

He barely acknowledged her question, just shrugging briefly without breaking off his blind contemplation of the small patch of the hospital grounds visible out of the window.

'Leo. . . Can I do anything to help?'

This time he did turn to look at her, and his eyes were so full of pain that she nearly cried out.

'No. . . No one can help,' he said, his voice sandpaper rough as if his throat were raw.

'Are you ill? Is it this flu bug that's going round?'

He chuckled, but there was no humour in it.

'I wish it was something that simple,' he murmured, and glanced at her again.

She had the sudden impression that he wanted to talk but, with the chance of others coming in very high, the staffroom definitely wasn't the best place.

'Do you want to go for a walk?' she suggested, unable to think of any other way they could guarantee seclusion.

He glanced significantly out at the dismal prospect and raised one eyebrow.

'Well, at least we'd have it to ourselves,' she pointed out with a tentative smile.

'On the assumption that the rest of the staff have too much sense to go out there?' he said, but she was pleased to see that, in spite of the resignation in his voice, he was getting to his feet.

Hannah dumped her coffee in the sink with hardly a glance. There would be other cups of coffee, but Leo needed her now.

'I'll grab my parka and meet you by the side-door,' she suggested, and crossed her fingers that she wasn't giving him time to regret his decision.

She breathed a sigh of relief when he joined her outside and, hands stuffed deep in pockets for warmth, they both began pacing slowly around the damp paths surrounding this end of the hospital buildings.

Hannah virtually had to resort to biting her tongue while she gave him time to decide whether he wanted to confide in her. She'd even begun to take note of the bank of shrubs they were passing which *hadn't* lost their foliage when he turned and began to pace towards the hospital again.

Her heart sank when she thought that the whole miserably chilly exercise had been a waste of time, but suddenly he halted and swung to face her.

'Do you ever wonder if it's all worthwhile?' he demanded quietly, his eyes darkly intent.

For just a second she was tempted to voice the sort of flippant reply she would give to any other questioner, but this was Leo and he was hurting.

The spiteful breeze flipped the ends of his tie up into the air but his reactions were too slow to prevent it flicking his face.

Hannah realised that it was still the same eye-catching composition he'd worn yesterday and he certainly didn't look as if he'd had much sleep since then. . .

'Often,' she admitted, finally answering his question. 'Some days all I seem to do is wonder whose stupid idea it was that I trained as a nurse.'

'And?' The word was almost a challenge.

'And then I have days when someone names their baby girl after me,' she reminded him with a wry grin. 'Somehow that seems to redress the balance.'

He closed his eyes and sighed deeply, his broad shoulders slumping as though from an insupportable weight.

'But what happens if there are too many bad days and not enough good? Too many days when you don't seem to be able to help enough people, too many people who are beyond helping?'

'And too little sleep. . .and too much stress. . .and not enough time to allow your soul to recover before the next onslaught,' Hannah enumerated with a sigh of her own.

There was silence between them then, but this time the air didn't contain the sharp-edged knives she'd felt before. This time Leo just seemed so. . .discouraged?

'Leo?' she began tentatively, then threw caution to the winds. 'Would a hug help?' she offered.

'A what?'

He blinked at her as if he had just woken from a strange dream.

'A hug,' she repeated, and hoped he would think the increased colour in her face was due to the sharpness of the wind.

Leo closed his eyes again, the smile which lifted the corners of his mouth almost painfully slow in appearing as he silently opened his arms.

'Oh, Hannah,' he murmured as she stepped closer and he wrapped them around her. 'You'll never know how much I needed this.'

CHAPTER SIX

'WHAT happened last night?' Hannah prompted softly from her position just under Leo's chin, his broad shoulders sheltering her easily from the chilly breeze.

He stiffened slightly as she broke the silence between them but she tightened her arms around his waist and burrowed her head deeper against him, as though she was settling in for the duration.

In fact, she had been quite prepared for him to make some excuse to push her away once the initial offer of a hug had been delivered, but he didn't move—almost as if he was weighing up his options.

Slowly she felt the tension drain out of him and he settled his arms more securely around her, one hand encircling her shoulders and the other nestling against the curve of her waist through the thick padding of her parka.

Under her ear she could hear the steady double beat of his heart and marvelled at the warmth and strength he radiated. He felt good. . .smelt good, in spite of the lingering hospital odour of antiseptic.

Today he seemed just a little rumpled around the edges but he'd obviously taken the time to shave, the fresh clean smell of the soap on his skin affecting her senses more than any artificial cologne—her breathing deepening unconsciously as she drew it into herself.

It had been so long since anything like this had happened that she'd almost forgotten how good it felt to be held like this. . .how easily it could help you to forget about all the miserable things happening in the world.

'A patient died last night,' he murmured in a husky voice, his words dragging her back to the real reason they were standing out here in the cold with their arms around each other.

The echo of pain was clear in the rough tone.

Hannah's heart jerked in response, then sank. She would never get used to the apparently senseless loss of life.

'One of the crash victims?'

She had a mental image of a very pregnant Sara as she had seen her last, and found herself surreptitiously crossing her fingers that nothing had happened to her or her baby.

'No. . .a young lad up in Birch Ward—ten years old.'

'Birch?' For a second she couldn't place the name—it wasn't one of the wards that A and E had much contact with. Then she remembered where it was—in the complex where cancer victims came to stay when they were undergoing courses of chemotherapy—and she nodded briefly to show she'd realised the significance.

'He had leukaemia.' Leo went on, and Hannah could have wept at the pain in his voice. 'We thought he'd beaten it—he seemed to be doing so well—but in the end. . .' He drew in a shuddering sigh.

'Was he a relative?' she asked. Perhaps the ten-year-old had been a nephew or even a young cousin.

'No, not a relative, but I'd known him for so long that it felt as if he should be part of the family. He was admitted the day after Lisa was.'

'Lisa?' A strange stab of jealousy forced her to ask, even though deep inside she didn't want to know who the woman was. Her intuition was telling her that she wasn't going to like the answer.

'My. . .my fiancée,' Leo said softly, hesitantly.

'Your. . .?' She stiffened, unable to say the
word as her heart turned into a lump of cold
lead inside her.

He had a fiancée? Leo was engaged—or at
least, he had been when he first met the young
lad who'd died last night?

She loosened her hold on him, feeling
strangely betrayed. When she would have
stepped back it was Leo's turn to tighten his
hold.

'She died three years ago, Hannah,' he murmured, his breath warm against her cheek, and
she felt suddenly guilty for the relief that
flashed through her—not relief that Lisa had
died, she hastily told herself, but relief that the
woman was no longer in Leo's life.

'How long had you known each other?' she
asked in a vain attempt at reminding herself
that *she* didn't have any place in Leo's life
either. They were colleagues—friends who
cared enough about each other to want to offer
comfort, but that was as far as it went. . .

'Most of my life, it seemed,' he said wryly.
'Her parents and mine were friends since before
they were married—they were my honorary

uncle and aunt throughout my childhood.'

Hannah stayed still and silent, knowing that he was far more likely to continue reminiscing if she didn't remind him that she was listening. In spite of the fact that the last thing she wanted to hear was how happy he and his Lisa had been, she knew instinctively that he needed to talk about it—especially after his young friend's death last night.

'She had just started planning the wedding when the leukaemia was diagnosed, but she swore both sets of parents to secrecy, hoping to get better before I found out.'

'What?' Her question was involuntary. How on earth had his fiancée thought she was going to hide something like that, and why would she *want* to hide it from the man she was going to marry?

'She wasn't involved in a medical career,' Leo explained wryly. 'She hadn't realised what sort of effect the chemo would have on her, nor could she have known that she would react so badly to it.'

He sighed softly, his attention focused on the pieces of gravel he was pushing around with the toe of his shoe while he retreated into the memories.

'I went to visit her,' he said, glancing up at her briefly. 'She was supposed to be staying with an old schoolfriend but her mother let something slip about visiting hours.'

He shook his head. 'They'd just told her that her only chance would be to have total body radiation and a bone-marrow graft, but all she could think about was the fact that she wouldn't be able to give me a family.'

He looked up at Hannah with anguish in his eyes.

'She told me to forget about her and find someone else, but there *wasn't* anyone else. . .I loved *her*.'

He shook his head as words momentarily failed him.

'I suggested bringing the date forward, but she insisted that the wedding couldn't take place until she was fit and well again. She wasn't going to walk up the aisle until she was looking her best—and certainly *not* with a wig on. . .'

Hannah hid a smile of admiration for the courageous woman and, as she listened to the rumble of his voice deep inside his chest, her initial petty jealousy died and was replaced by the wish that she could have met her. Leo deserved someone like his Lisa in his life. . .

'What happened?' Hannah asked, finally daring to lift her head from its comfortable resting place to look up at him. She knew that Leo wasn't likely to stop telling her the story at this point, and for some unexplained reason she felt she needed to see his expression while he was talking about Lisa.

He was looking out over her head, his whisky-coloured eyes staring blindly at the lacklustre scenery around them—as if his whole concentration was on the events inside his head.

'We couldn't get her into remission and she went downhill quite rapidly.' He drew in a deep sigh and finally looked down into her upturned face. His eyes were dark with painful memories and Hannah's heart clenched with the helpless need to comfort him.

'As the original date of the wedding drew closer she became very depressed. Her parents even approached the hospital chaplain about the possibility of conducting the wedding on the ward but she wouldn't hear of it.' His brief chuckle owed little to humour and sounded as if it had been forced past a huge obstruction in his chest.

'She said. . .she said I was far too young to be a widower and far too good-looking and, anyway, she'd lost so much weight that she'd look terrible in her wedding dress—like a scarecrow. . .'

His words ended on a whisper and because she could see he was fighting tears she looked away to give him some small measure of privacy—as much as she could with his arms wrapped so tightly around her.

She heard him swallow heavily before he began to speak again, his voice sounding almost rusty in the chilly air.

'I spent so much time on the ward with her that I got to know the regulars quite well—there's a special atmosphere up there that you rarely find on any other ward.'

Hannah smiled. She'd spent part of her training on a children's ward, and she knew what Leo meant about the atmosphere there.

'Simon was one of the ones who looked as if he was going to make it—until his blood count a month ago. I've visited him most days—partly to give his parents a break together—and I was just about to go home at the end of my shift last night when he sent a message down that he wanted to see me.'

'And you went up and sat with him,' Hannah guessed as everything fell into place.

In spite of her efforts at maintaining a sensible emotional distance between the two of them, she had learned so much more about Leo Stirling than she'd known on the night of the Autumn Ball. . .certainly enough to know that he had willingly given up a night's sleep to keep his young friend company during his last few hours.

The strident sound of an approaching ambulance shattered the silent bond which had wound its way between them, and the outside world reappeared around them.

Suddenly realising that she still had her arms wrapped around him, Hannah loosened her hold on his waist and tried awkwardly to step back.

Leo resisted for a moment, pulling her back against his lean length for one last squeeze.

'Hannah?'

The hesitant tone in his voice drew her eyes up to meet his again in spite of the embarrassment which coloured her cheeks when she realised how their embrace would be interpreted should anyone see them. She'd been so isolated within the little cocoon they'd woven around themselves that it had taken the sound of the siren to make her see what they had been doing.

She could only be grateful for the bank of evergreen shrubs which had screened them from prying eyes—she certainly hadn't been thinking about the effect it could have on their reputations.

'Thank you,' Leo said sincerely, his slow attempt at a smile a painful imitation of his usual ladykiller grin—but it still managed to jump-start her pulse rate. 'Thank you for listening. . .for being there for me.'

'There's no need for thanks,' she began, conscious that she was trying to dismiss his effect on her senses as much as deflect his gratitude.

'Ah, but there is,' he insisted, his hands gripping her shoulders as he towered over her. 'Double thanks, in fact. Once from me, for allowing me to weep all over your shoulder, and once from the department, who will now be able to work with me for the rest of my shift without fear of being shouted at in spite of doing their best.'

The expression in his eyes matched the sincerity in his tone and she had to fight the prickle of response in her own eyes.

'S-so,' she said on a shaky breath, 'I'm responsible for pulling the thorn out of Leo the Lion's paw for the sake of peace in the jungle?'

After a startled second of silence Leo threw his head back in a quick burst of appreciative laughter.

'Now, isn't that just typical of you, Hannah?' he said with a chuckle as he turned her back towards the side-entrance they'd used at the beginning of their break.

In spite of the fact that they were now in full view of anyone who bothered to look out of the window, he wrapped his arm around her shoulders and pulled her close to his side for a one-armed hug.

It wasn't until they were walking back along the path that she realised how cold her feet were. She hadn't noticed all the while they were talking but suddenly she was worried about how long they'd spent outside. Was she going to be late back on duty?

She fished inside her parka for the watch pinned to the front of her uniform and was surprised to see how little time had actually passed since they'd come outside—it seemed as if they'd been talking for hours if the amount of ground they'd covered was anything to go by.

'Whatever happens,' Leo said as he pushed the door open for her and ushered her into the enveloping warmth of the hospital building, 'you always seem to manage to come up smiling.'

Hannah was glad he couldn't see her face when his final words registered.

Not always, she thought sadly as she hurried to put her parka away. There had been times, over the last couple of years, when it had taken every bit of acting ability she possessed not to break down and cry, regardless of where she was or who might be watching.

Sometimes it was only the thought that there were other people in far worse situations which kept her going.

Sternly she pushed the unhappy memories into their dark corner in the back of her mind and set off towards the main reception area. If the noise of sirens was anything to go by, she would soon be too busy to think about anything other than her job.

'Sister Nicholls,' a familiar Scottish voice called almost as soon as she appeared through the doors.

'Yes, Sister.' Hannah hurried across, knowing the tone denoted urgency.

'Will you take Michelle through to three? She's been vomiting for nearly eighteen hours. I'll send Dr Stirling as soon as possible.'

The young girl sitting in the wheelchair had so little colour in her face she looked almost grey. Her skin was sheened with sweat and her pale silky hair was plastered to her head.

'Mum, *I* want to have a go in the wheelchair. Why is *she* having all the rides?' whined a petulant voice just behind her, and Hannah glanced briefly in its direction then blinked.

If it hadn't been for the fact that the whinging child had so much more colour in his face, the two of them would be indistinguishable. The likeness was too marked for them to be anything other than twins.

'Are you Michelle's mother?' she asked, pausing only briefly on her way to the examining room. 'Do you want to follow me?'

The offer was just a formality because most parents would fight to be allowed to accompany their children when they were ill.

'Oh, no.' The overweight woman's chins wobbled as she shook her head and glared in her daughter's direction while she put a comforting hand on her son's shoulder.

'Poor Michael doesn't like seeing people being sick—I'm certain she's only doing it because she knows it upsets him. I told her to stop it last night when she made a mess of her bed, but she didn't take any notice. Selfish, that's what she is, just plain selfish. . .'

As Hannah wheeled her charge swiftly away from the rambling diatribe she had to press her lips tightly together to prevent herself from telling the stupid woman what she thought of her.

There was no way this frail angel of a child could have deliberately made herself sick for eighteen hours. The strongest will in the world couldn't have made her bring herself to such a state of collapse, nor have given her such a high temperature.

'She's badly dehydrated,' Leo confirmed when he arrived a couple of minutes later. 'Get an IV going as soon as possible to get some fluids into her.'

He continued his examination, gently questioning their apathetic patient and trying to tease her into some sort of a response, but she was obviously too overwhelmed by everything that was happening to her.

'Ouch!' Her cry of distress was hardly more than a mew as Leo palpated her abdomen, her enormous blue eyes swimming in tears.

'Positive McBurney's. . .acute,' he muttered after he'd soothed their little patient with a heartfelt apology for having to hurt her, then grabbed for a bowl and held it for her while she retched helplessly.

Hannah took over, wiping the girl's pasty little face with a cool cloth as Leo strode across to the phone and tapped out the code to connect him to Theatre.

While he was arranging for Michelle to go straight up for prepping Hannah mentally patted herself on the back that her own diagnosis of a badly inflamed appendix had been confirmed.

Now they needed to get her ready to go up as quickly as possible, and that included getting her awful mother to sign the parental consent for the operation.

'I don't understand it,' Hannah told Tina when they were finally freed for a coffee-break. 'That woman has the most beautiful set of twins and she seems to be lavishing all her love and attention on one of them and ignoring the other.'

'How's the little girl doing? Did we get her on the table in time?' her young colleague questioned with concern.

'Only just,' Hannah confirmed with a shudder when she remembered the message relayed from Theatre. 'Her appendix was already gangrenous when they opened her up. If her mother had left her suffering for another few hours it could have perforated, and it might even have been too late to do anything.'

'Well, all I can say is thank goodness we sometimes get lighter moments,' Tina commented when Hannah subsided a little. 'Did you hear about Mrs Myfanwy Griffiths?'

Hannah shook her head. 'A patient this afternoon?' she asked. She was still angry about events earlier but was willing to have her attention diverted.

'Yes. A Welsh lady with a very pronounced accent,' Tina said with a creditable imitation. 'She was in a lot of pain—apparently she'd probably passed a gallstone and she's been sent up so they can look for more.'

'Don't tell me—she was fair, fat, female, fertile, forty, feverish and flatulent,' Hannah enumerated, counting the well-known indicators on her fingers.

'Very!' Tina agreed with a laugh. 'She was talking nineteen-to-the-dozen, telling us about the concert she had been hoping to go to tonight while Dr Stirling was palpating her abdomen. Suddenly she released a noisy gust of wind and she went purple with embarrassment.'

'The poor woman,' Hannah said with a chuckle.

'That's not the best of it,' Tina said, really getting into her stride. 'Dr Stirling said to her, "Was that Purcell's Trumpet Voluntary?" and she said, quick as a flash, "No, Doctor, more like Griffiths's Trumpet *In*voluntary!"'

An appreciative laugh ran around the room, everyone's attention having been caught by Tina's clever imitation of Mrs Griffith's Welsh accent.

The silly story had finally taken the edge off Hannah's anger and she was idly looking towards the clock on the wall when she did a horrified double-take. If she didn't get moving she was going to be late for her appointment.

As she hurried through the hospital she couldn't help a wry chuckle at the realisation that she had been so wrapped up in the events in the department that afternoon that she'd almost managed to miss the appointment which had been hanging over her like a big black cloud for the last few days.

Now remembrance returned with the force of a tsunami, obliterating everything in its path.

Hannah pushed open the door of the department, conscious for the first that her hand was visibly shaking.

A quick glance around the empty waiting area told her that she wouldn't have long to wait—at least the consultant was sensitive enough to realise how stressful these appointments were and made certain there was as little hanging around as possible.

Half an hour later it was all over for another six months, but her hands were still trembling when she returned to the department.

Hannah had surprised herself by confiding the nature of her appointment to Celia MacDonald when she'd asked for permission to leave the department. Her superior hadn't asked for details but had been concerned that she ought to go home when she'd finished, but Hannah had been adamant that she would far rather be kept busy.

Anyway, she thought as she reported back, there was only another hour to the end of her shift.

She was just in time to take her turn to stand on the apron of the emergency entrance as another ambulance reversed swiftly towards her, the doors flying open almost before the vehicle was stationary.

'OD,' Ted Larrabee said crisply as he unlocked the trolley and pulled it towards himself with an expertise which spoke of much practice. 'Female, name unknown, age approximately early thirties,' he continued, while his colleague concentrated on the rhythmic count of resuscitation. 'She's taken a complete cocktail, by the look of those. . .' He pointed at the plastic bag beside the ominously still body and the assortment of bottles visible inside.

Hannah found herself running along beside the trolley as the young woman was whisked through, and she briefly crossed her fingers and sent up a prayer for their unhappy patient as the team swung into its horribly familiar routine.

They did everything they could, working hard to save the life of someone who apparently hadn't valued it herself, but it was all in vain.

It wasn't until Hannah had time to go through the clothes they'd taken off her to see if she could find some sort of identification that she found the note.

'Leo, I've found something,' she called as she began to read. 'Her name was Tamsin French and. . . Oh, God. . .' she finished on a whisper when she turned the piece of paper over and found the reason for the young woman's suicide.

Suddenly there was a strange buzzing sound in her head and the room seemed to go slightly out of focus.

As if from a great distance, she could hear Leo calling her name and she could see him coming towards her, but he almost seemed to be moving in slow motion as her knees refused to hold her weight any longer and she sank silently into darkness.

'Hannah?' called an insistent voice. 'Hannah, can you hear me? Open your eyes, now.'

It was an effort just to lift her eyelids when she would far rather have stayed in the silent anonymity of the dark. Something told her that she wasn't going to like what she found out when she woke up properly, but that voice was accustomed to being obeyed.

'Good girl,' Celia MacDonald said briskly when Hannah finally peered up at her. 'How are you feeling?'

Hannah blinked and tried to sit up.

'Now, then, you know better than that,' the senior sister chided as she put a firm hand on her shoulder and pushed her back down. 'Just stay still for a moment until you catch your breath.'

She subsided, horrified by how weak and shaky she felt. What on earth had happened to her to make her feel so. . .?

'Oh, Lord,' she groaned as her lapsed memory returned in glorious Technicolor. 'Please. . .tell me I didn't faint.'

'I could tell you but it wouldn't be true,' retorted the bustling little figure as she trapped Hannah's wrist in expert fingers and counted her pulse without a pause in the conversation.

'You went out like the proverbial light. It was a good job Dr Stirling was quick on his feet or you'd be sporting a fine crop of bruises.'

Hannah groaned again as she remembered her impression that Leo was walking towards her in slow motion. He must have been moving a great deal faster than she'd thought if he'd managed to catch her before she'd hit the floor.

'I knew you should have gone home after your appointment,' her superior said, dropping her voice so that she wouldn't break confidentiality. 'That's not the sort of thing you can easily shrug off—far too much stress involved.'

'It. . .it wasn't that,' Hannah said, stumbling to her own defence. 'It was the suicide they brought in.'

'What? That young woman? Was she a friend of yours?'

'No, but she had just been diagnosed with cancer.'

Hannah knew she didn't have to say any more when she saw comprehension dawn on Celia MacDonald's face.

'Och, lass. I'm sorry.'

'How is she feeling now?' interrupted Leo as he strode across the examining room. 'Any idea why she keeled over, Sister?'

Hannah's eyes zeroed in on his face. How long had he been there? How much of their conversation had he heard?

'It was probably a combination of reasons, the way it usually is,' the senior sister said diplomatically. 'But, whatever the reason, it's time she went home.'

'Well, as I've already handed over to Nick, I'm just the person to make sure she gets there safely,' Leo declared as he offered Hannah a hand to help her to sit up. 'Take it slowly until you're sure you aren't going to flake out on us again.'

'I don't need someone to follow me home,' Hannah said, horribly aware of the petulant tone in her voice, but her emotions were in such turmoil that she was almost afraid to spend too much time in his company.

'No, you need someone to *take* you home— don't you think so, Sister?' Leo demanded evenly, his eyes far too intent for her peace of mind.

Hannah glared at him for enlisting her senior's agreement. There was no way she could go against both of them and he knew it.

'So, what was all that about?' Leo demanded.

He'd hardly given her time to fasten her seat belt before he drove away and already the inquisition had begun.

'All what?' she queried cautiously—there was no way she was going to volunteer information unless it was strictly unavoidable.

'Oh, come on, Hannah,' he snapped. 'You've been as jumpy as a cat on hot bricks for half the day, then you disappear for some mysterious appointment and almost as soon as you come back you pass out.'

That was one way of putting the facts together, she supposed. At least it meant that he hadn't heard enough of her conversation with Celia MacDonald to make a connection with the unfortunate woman who'd committed. . .

'And what was that business with the suicide note?' he continued, blowing *that* idea to smithereens and winding the tension up another notch as she searched frantically for a way to explain the inexplicable.

Why did the man have to be so sharp-witted?

She'd just been getting used to the idea that they could be friends, but if he forced her to tell him. . . She sighed heavily. She knew that everything would change. . .again. . .and she'd be left alone and hurting. . .again.

'Please, Hannah, talk to me,' he said into the darkness of the car, his voice calmer and more even now, as though he'd managed to find a degree of control.

'Oh, Leo. . .' She blinked furiously to beat back the threat of tears, saddened by the fact that she couldn't confide in him.

Since Laura had fallen in love with Wolff their friendship had altered, and Leo had slowly become the closest friend she had but even so. . .

Leo parked the car outside the front of her house and she reached for the seat belt release, but before she could use it he'd turned towards her and rested one hand over hers to hold her still.

'Hannah. . .are you pregnant?' he asked softly.

'Wh-what? No!' she squeaked in horror. 'Of course I'm not pregnant, Leo.'

'Then what *is* it?' he demanded, one fist thumping the steering-wheel. 'You went white as a sheet and crumpled into a heap. There must be *something* the matter.'

He caught her hand and cradled it between both of his, rubbing it gently as if she needed warming.

'Please, Hannah, I'm worried about you. I. . .I care about you.' He lifted her hand and brushed a gentle kiss over her knuckles.

The sweetness and unexpectedness of the caress was her undoing, an electric shiver travelling over every nerve ending as she fought for control.

How could she ignore the thread of hurt in his concern when deep inside she longed to be able to speak openly about the things going on in her life? But, equally, how could she bear it if she confided in him and ruined their fledgeling friendship?

Was there some way she could tell him enough of her history so that he would understand the nightmares which haunted her, the way she'd told Celia MacDonald only as much as she *needed* to know?

Almost unconsciously she wove her fingers between his and returned the pressure, her decision made. If she had to carry the burden alone much longer she really would be in danger of going round the bend.

'It was the young woman committing suicide which blew my fuse,' she began in a shaky voice, but she was pleased to hear that it became stronger with each word.

'I've. . .I've already lost four members of my family to cancer—my grandmother, my mother and two aunts. I'm. . .' She had to pause for a deep breath before she could continue. 'I'm the last one left,' she finished on a whisper, her lips quivering uncontrollably.

'Oh, God, Hannah, I'm sorry,' Leo said as he tried to gather her into his arms for comfort, but the seat belt thwarted him.

Hannah sat there with tears slowly dripping off the edge of her chin as he found the release and triggered it, then he paused and cradled one wet cheek in his palm.

'It's my turn to give *you* a hug this time,' he said determinedly. 'And as I can't to do it in the front seat of a car you're going to have to let me into your flat.'

Hannah's breath caught in her throat at the thought of Leo coming into her flat, and she stared up at him in the darkness of the car with silent tears still sliding down her cheeks.

Her emotions see-sawed between excitement and fear but most of all she realised that she needed to be held, needed the comfort of Leo's strong arms around her, even if it was just for a short while.

'A-all right,' she whispered as she swiped at her tears with shaky hands, before fumbling for the doorhandle. 'I—I could make you a cup of coffee, if you like.'

His murmured reply was lost in the sound of opening car doors and she could only presume that he'd agreed.

The wind had grown much colder and the remains of her tears felt icy on her cheeks as she hurried to the main door and tried to fit the key in the lock.

'Here, let me,' Leo offered gently when her third failure started the tears falling again and he took over the task.

'I'm upstairs,' she whispered as she gestured towards the stairwell. 'It. . .it's not as convenient as a ground floor flat, but it does mean that I don't have to put up with other people's feet stamping about over my head. . .I'm sorry. . .you've already been there and. . .and I'm so wound up I'm babbling like an idiot. . .'

She bit her lip and sniffed helplessly as he used the other key to unlock her front door and ushered her into the softly lit hallway with a solicitous arm around her shoulders.

'Don't worry about it, my love,' he murmured as he leant back against the door to close it behind them, and pulled her into his arms. 'I think you can be forgiven for babbling today.'

My love? Had he really called her 'my love'?

The endearment was so sweet and so unexpected that it dried her tears and she stared up at him speechlessly, startled by how easily he'd said the word.

'Ah, Hannah, we both know how it hurts,' he whispered as he cradled her head against

his shoulder and tightened his arms around her.
'We know what it's like to watch the ones we
love fading away when their bodies just can't
fight any more, and we know what the loneliness is like when they're gone...to want
someone to hold you and tell you the hurt will
go away...'

'Does it ever go away?' she whispered
brokenly. 'Don't you just carry it with you for
ever, with each new generation going through
the same fear and torment?'

'Ah, shh, Hannah, shh.'

He framed her face between his palms and
brushed his lips over hers as though to banish
her words.

Hannah froze at the intimate contact, her
breath trapped in her throat.

CHAPTER SEVEN

'HANNAH?' Leo whispered, the word a simple question as his breath flowed warm against her chilled skin.

Hannah's eyes were drawn upwards, widening when she saw the expression on his face— a haunting mixture of desire and desperation.

'A hug isn't enough this time, is it?' he breathed. 'I want to kiss you. . . I *need* to kiss you. . .'

As he wrapped his arms even tighter around her and pulled her between his spread thighs she discovered the unmistakable evidence that he was heavily aroused, and she drew in a shuddering breath.

Her own body softened in response and she leant helplessly against him, her head tilting back and her lips parting in surrender without a conscious decision.

'Do you want me to kiss you?' he whispered, and she gazed drowsily up at him out of half-closed eyes at lips poised just millimetres from her own as if he wanted to tease her to death.

'Hannah, I need to hear you say it,' he demanded hoarsely. 'Do you want it as much as I do?'

It was his intensity which helped her to find the last of her reserves of strength as she slid her hands up behind his head and speared her fingers through the silky strands of his hair to cup the curve of his skull.

'Yes. . .' she hissed as she surged against him and tightened her grasp on the back of his head to close the final distance between them.

It was never like this before, she thought in a flash of ecstatic revelation as lips slid sensuously over lips and tongues duelled in the heated darkness. Until this moment no one has ever made me feel as if they were the other half of my soul, as essential to my life as air or water.

As if the move had been choreographed by years of intimate knowledge, their hands were mapping each other's contours—the intimidating breadth of his shoulders and the trim slenderness of her waist, the muscular strength of his back and the sleek curve of her hip.

And yet it wasn't enough.

As tightly as they were wrapped in each other's arms, they couldn't get close enough or kiss deeply enough to satisfy the desire which soared out of control.

'Please,' he whispered, his breath searing her lips with heat and his hands delving beneath the hem of her uniform to slide up the silky length of her trembling thighs.

At first he seemed content just to cup her bottom in his hands and pull her against his own body, and Hannah revelled in the sensations, her body rocking against his and savouring the evidence of his desire for her.

Suddenly it wasn't enough and impatience took over as his hands tried to find a way through her underwear to make contact with her naked skin.

Hannah stilled for just a second as she realised what he was doing, but then she realised with a jolt of excitement and acceptance that she wanted it just as much and leant back just far enough to allow him to reach his objective.

'Ah, Hannah,' he groaned when she shyly took advantage of the change in position to deliver caresses of her own, her hands tentatively exploring his heat through the fine fabric of his trousers.

Soon she felt the same impatience, and it

was the work of seconds to find the tab of his
zip. Even though her fingers were trembling it
slid down easily to allow her access to explore
yet more intimately.

For just a second, as his heat branded itself
into her cool hand, he stood stock-still and gave
an agonised groan. Hannah froze in the middle
of her fascinated exploration, suddenly afraid
that she'd displeased him.

She looked up at him. . .up into tiger-bright
eyes which seared her to her soul with the
demanding intensity of their golden fire, and
when she realised that his breathing was as
laboured as if he'd been running a race she
understood for the first time just how tightly
he had been controlling his desire.

For wordless moments they gazed into each
other's eyes and then she moved her hand
again, encompassing his quivering length in a
graphic answer to his unspoken question.

Desire exploded between them as they tore
at each other's clothes, unable to wait once the
decision had been made, doing nothing more
than removing the bare necessities of clothing
to allow their bodies to merge in that ultimate
communion.

For a single instant Hannah was conscious

of the fact that Leo had been so impatient that he'd torn her tights away, and that she'd wrenched the button off the waistband of his expensive trousers to pull them down his straining thighs...but then he had wrapped his powerful hands around her hips and lifted her up against him, before holding her in the perfect position for his fierce thrust.

'Leo...!' she cried as all the breath was forced out of her lungs in an explosive rush, and he froze.

'Oh, God, Hannah, did I hurt you?' he demanded in tones of anguish, and the muscles in his shoulders and arms contracted as he began to lift her.

'No...' she groaned, and wrapped her legs tightly around his slim hips, trying to tighten her arms around his neck. 'Don't take it away...'

She felt his ribs jerk as he chuckled and then he pressed his forehead against hers.

'To tell you the truth, I don't think I could,' he whispered as he allowed her to pull them tightly together again. 'It feels too good, being like this, to want to move at all.'

Hannah knew what he meant and wreathed her arms around his shoulders to maintain the ultimate closeness between them, revelling in the fact that the two of them were as united as a man and woman could be.

She also knew the moment when just being close wasn't enough, and the warning spasms in the nerves and muscles deep inside her drew answering twitches from the tumescent member buried there that the need to move was growing uncontrollable.

'You're doing that on purpose,' Leo growled as he palmed her bottom and tried to stop her moving by pulling her tightly against himself, but it was as much use as trying to stop an earthquake.

The closer their bodies were the closer they wanted to be, and in the end the apparently haphazard friction gave way to the driving rhythm which could only have one result.

'Oh, Hannah, I'm sorry,' she heard Leo groan when he finally draw a deep enough breath to speak.

'Sorry?' Hannah repeated in a whisper as her heart clenched inside her and she awkwardly began to unwind herself from around him.

She was suddenly distressingly aware that to an outside observer it would look as if they

hadn't bothered to do any more than uncover
their sexual organs before they'd coupled like
ravenous animals.

How was it possible to go from ecstatic
closeness to uncomfortable vulnerability in the
space of seconds, without shattering into a mil-
lion fragments? If, after the most earth-shaking
experience of her life, all he felt were regrets. . .

'Hey! Where are you going?' he demanded
indignantly as he refused to loosen his hold,
maintaining the contact between them.

'But. . .' Hannah stilled self-consciously,
feeling a bit like a butterfly on a pin. 'You
said. . .'

She was confused. He'd apologised. . .
sounded so full of regret. . .but when she'd
tried to leave him he'd stopped her.

Had she misunderstood?

Didn't he want her to go?

There was only one way to find out.

'Why did you say you were sorry?' she
demanded, bravely meeting his eyes with her
own.

'Well, it certainly *wasn't* because I regretted
what just happened between us, if that's what
you were thinking,' he declared fervently. 'My
only regret was that it happened too fast for any

sort of consideration or finesse!' He glanced around at her dimly lit hallway and gave a disbelieving laugh. 'I hardly let you get inside your front door, for heaven's sake!'

A flood of relief immersed Hannah in new warmth and she tightened her hold around his neck. Her spirits rose like a helium balloon on a hot day and tempted her to a teasing retort.

'There are those who might say that I hardly let you get inside my front door before I leapt on you,' she pointed out, and revelled in his sensuous chuckle as she buried her face against the warmth of his neck to revel in the scent of his continuing sexual arousal.

'Shall we give it another try?' he whispered against her ear, as if he was sensitive to the direction of her thoughts, his lips caressing her even as he spoke. 'How about starting off with a bit of novelty and undressing each other before we go any further?'

He tightened his hands suggestively around her bottom and arched himself against her, as if to remind her that they were still intimately joined. 'I can't wait to see all those curves I've been admiring for so long.'

Her renewed awareness of his body inside hers nearly prevented her from hearing his final words, but once they registered in her brain everything came to a screeching halt.

'Wh-what?' she gasped, suddenly cold and trembling inside at the thought that he wanted this encounter to continue. It wouldn't have been so bad—in fact, it would have been fantastic—if he'd only wanted an action replay of the explosive encounter they'd just enjoyed.

Unfortunately Leo naturally wanted variations on the theme, and that just wasn't possible.

Hannah cringed at the thought of having Leo take the rest of her clothes off and fear sent her pulse into overdrive.

What could she say?

How could she tell him that this utterly intoxicating episode was all there could ever be between them without telling him why?

'Hey! You haven't gone to sleep on me, have you?' he chided huskily as he nuzzled her temple, and she nearly hugged him with relief as she realised that he had just handed her the perfect excuse.

'Hmm?' she murmured with just the right amount of sleepy question in the sound.

'Oh, Hannah, you're hell on my ego,' he complained softly as he brushed a tender kiss over her cheek. Hannah kept her eyes tightly closed but his gentleness filled her chest with an enormous ache as he shifted her in his arms and carried her carefully through to her bedroom.

She couldn't help the way her body tensed when he deposited her on her bed, and she rolled away from him and wrapped her arms defensively around herself as though subconsciously conserving heat.

'Hey, sweetheart,' he coaxed. 'Let me help you get undressed. . .'

She feigned oblivion and sighed silently when he quickly gave up the attempt, having to content himself with sliding the covers out from under her and tucking them around her apparently sleeping body.

'Good night, my love,' she heard him whisper as he smoothed one hand over her tousled hair. 'I'll see you tomorrow.'

Over the erratic thumping of her heart Hannah heard him move through her flat, and even imagined she could hear him retrieving his scattered clothing in her tiny hallway before there was the very final sound of the lock catching as he shut her front door behind him.

Safe in the knowledge that he'd finally gone,

she rolled over and lay staring up at the ceiling as the full horror of the situation poured over her.

She'd just made love with St Augustine's A and E department's resident heart-throb, Leo Stirling, the first man she'd made love to since Jonathan broke their engagement—the first man she'd even *noticed* as a man since then— and suddenly she realised that her life was made up of two inescapable truths.

The first was that, in spite of her determination not to let anyone get so close to her that she became emotionally involved with them, she had fallen in love with Leo and every exasperating, irrepressible enigma that he'd turned out to be.

The second truth was the one which made her newly vulnerable heart feel like lead—that she was never going to be able to do anything about her love.

She sighed deeply as she accepted that final inescapable fact and rolled over again to curl herself up in a tight ball under the warmth of her thick duvet.

A taunting voice inside her head told her that it wasn't as warm or as comforting as Leo's strong arms would be, but she firmly ignored it, banishing the erotic mental images of the two of them generating enough heat not to *need* a duvet over them.

She didn't have time for such heated imaginings.

What she had to do now was rack her brains for some way of facing him in the morning. Playing possum tonight might have put off the evil hour, but she had no doubt that Leo wouldn't be content to leave it at that.

'All right, poppet, all right,' Hannah crooned as she tried to soothe the unhappy child in her arms. She'd managed to take his clothes off, but he didn't seem to want to allow himself be wrapped up in a blanket by some strange woman and kept trying to struggle out of her grasp.

'I know you're feeling rotten, sweetheart,' his mother said as she stroked a consoling hand over his head, 'but the nurse is going to see what she can do about it as soon as possible.'

'Good morning.'

While her young patient's worried parents swung towards the deep-voiced pleasantry, Hannah found herself stiffening devensively.

Even without looking, she knew that the man

behind her was unmistakably Leo, and it was the first time she'd seen him today. . .the first time since she'd feigned sleep in his arms. . .

'Good morning, Doctor,' she began endless seconds later when she finally forced herself to turn to face him with the unhappy child still in her arms.

She was horribly conscious that the quiver in her voice was probably audible to everyone in the room, and a slow heat crawled its way up into her cheeks.

'This is Liam O'Malley and his parents. He's eighteen months old and he's had five days of fever, rash, vomiting and swollen glands. They've been to their GP several times, but Liam's no better and they're beginning to get very worried about him.'

As usual, Leo paused to crouch down to his little patient's level to pull a funny face and smile at him. He'd told Hannah long ago that he believed such direct contact was invaluable when the time came for him to actually need to do something to the child because he had already begun a form of communication between them.

'Hey, big boy, aren't you feeling so good?' he demanded as he gently smoothed one palm over the child's head and stroked the back of a finger over his cheek. 'Shall I ask your mummy and daddy what's been going on?'

He straightened up and stepped back to introduce himself to the young couple.

'I'm Dr Stirling, Mr and Mrs O'Malley. Can you tell me what's been happening the last few days? When did Liam become sick? Which symptoms arrived first?'

Hannah could see from their body language that the two of them were under a great deal of stress, her hand clutched tightly in his as though they were afraid they might fall apart if they didn't hold onto each other.

As if it wasn't bad enough that their child wasn't well, Hannah realised from their recounting of the events of the last few days that repeated visits to their GP hadn't seemed to have brought them any closer to knowing what was wrong with Liam, nor what needed to be done about it.

'The first time we took him he was a little bit warm and he'd been sick. The doctor told us to give him a liquid painkiller and said that he was probably teething,' Mr O'Malley told them. 'We took his word for it because they're supposed to know—'

'He more or less told us that we were making a fuss over nothing,' his wife broke in, 'but when his glands kept getting bigger and he still had a temperature we took him back twice. He finally decided to give us an antibiotic for him and said it was a simple infection or inflammation—probably something to do with his ears.'

'Did that help him?' Leo asked as he gently felt around Liam's jaw. Standing so close to him, Hannah could see the slight frown which pleated his forehead and knew he'd found the enlarged glands too.

She flicked back one layer of the enveloping blanket, knowing that he would be wanting to check other sites on Liam's body such as those in his armpits and groin.

'It didn't seem to make any difference,' Mrs O'Malley said as her anxious eyes tracked his every move.

'In fact,' her husband continued, 'he'd started developing other symptoms by then.'

'Such as?' Leo prompted as he continued his exploration.

'As you can see, his hands and feet are very red and swollen—it almost looks as if he's got inflated rubber gloves on—and his mouth started to get red and sore and now it's gone cracked and bleeding.'

'How long have his eyes been this red?' As Leo thumbed back the lids, Hannah could see just how bloodshot they were and was quite horrified—she'd never seen anything like it before, especially on a child this young.

'Must be nearly three days now,' Mrs O'Malley confirmed. 'And the skin on his hands and feet just doesn't feel right—it seems all dry and leathery.'

'Have any tests been done?'

'Not so far.' Mr O'Malley scowled. 'The GP said that as it obviously wasn't meningitis it was a waste of time and money doing tests on babies this young because by the time the results came through they had invariably recovered and were up and running around again as right as rain.'

'We weren't happy with that,' his wife added. 'So finally he said if Liam wasn't any better by the beginning of next week he might send him to the hospital for a lumbar puncture. . . Doctor, is that because it might be meningitis after all? There's been such a lot about it on the television the last few years, but they always say that you should take your child to the doctor straight away.'

'You're quite right.' Leo glanced up from his careful examination of little Liam's peeling feet with a quick smile. 'If you think your child might have meningitis it's *essential* to make the diagnosis quickly, but I'm almost certain that your doctor got it right—that Liam *hasn't* got meningitis.'

'Thank God for that,' muttered Mr O'Malley, and Hannah saw the quick glance he threw his equally worried wife. 'Do you have any idea what *is* the matter with him?'

'Yes, I'm fairly certain that I do,' he said as he straightened up with a smile. 'If you'd like to take a seat for a minute, I'm just going to telephone Great Ormond Street Hospital. There's a friend of mine there and he's made this his special interest. I'd like to speak to him for confirmation, and then I'll be straight back.'

His long legs took him swiftly out of the room, and Hannah took pity on the two of them as they hovered uneasily, their eyes travelling helplessly between their child and the door as it swung silently closed behind the departing doctor.

'Mrs O'Malley, would you like to perch yourself on the edge of the trolley and give

Liam a cuddle while we're waiting for Dr Stirling to come back? The little chap's been very good for us so far, but I think he'd be much happier if it was his mum holding him.'

The poor woman almost leapt at the chance to have him in her own arms again, and the way her husband stood close enough to run a gentle finger over his little son's downy dark hair told Hannah how much he loved the boy.

Leo would be like that, she thought, the words surfacing in her head from nowhere. He would be the sort of father who liked to hold and stroke his children. . .to cuddle them and tease them. . .

She gave her head a single fierce shake to rid herself of the impossible dream that they would be *her* children Leo would be treating so lovingly, and made herself concentrate on checking that the child's notes were complete.

'Right, Mr and Mrs O'Malley, we're in business!' Leo declared as he strode back into the room with a pleased smile on his face. 'We're ninety-nine per cent certain that we know what's the matter with Liam and, if he's only been sick for five days, it's been caught in time.'

'What is it, Doctor?' Mr O'Malley seemed

utterly bemused by the tall doctor's ebullient attitude. 'What's the matter with my boy?'

'It's called Kawasaki disease,' Leo announced, as if he were pulling a rabbit out of a hat, and Hannah felt a smile of comprehension curl up the corners of her mouth as she recognised the name.

'Kawasaki?' questioned Mrs O'Malley. 'But. . .that's the name of a motorbike, isn't it?'

'Quite right,' Leo confirmed with a smile. 'But it's also the name of a disease little children can suffer from.'

'Is it a new one—one of these superbugs?' her husband asked fearfully. 'Are they still trying to find a cure for it?'

'It's relatively new—it was first described about thirty years ago—but, providing it's caught in the first ten days and the right treatment given in time, we're over ninety per cent successful with it.'

'What *is* the treatment? Is it very painful?' Mrs O'Malley tightened her arms around her little son protectively. 'And what would happen if he didn't get it in time?'

'If he doesn't receive the treatment in the first ten days there's a thirty per cent chance that the disease can cause serious heart damage because it attacks the arteries around the heart and causes weak patches that can blow up like balloons. Eventually it can cause heart failure.'

'And the treatment?' prompted Mr O'Malley, his face suddenly ashen at the thought of such things happening to their precious son.

'It's as easy to administer as a blood transfusion,' Leo explained with a reassuring smile. 'In fact, what we'll be putting into his vein is just one part of what naturally occurs in whole blood. It's called gamma globulin—it's one of the plasma proteins and contains high levels of antibodies.'

'How long will it be before you can start the treatment? Does it take a long time?' The young mother was a different person altogether now, her tension all directed towards getting the treatment started.

'It will take a few minutes to sort out all the formalities to admit Liam to the ward, but once he's up there...'

'Admit him?' she interrupted fearfully. 'Oh, Doctor, can't you do it here so we can be with him?'

'There's nothing to worry about, Mrs O'Malley,' Leo soothed with a liberal application of his famous smile. 'You can go up with him and stay while the gamma globulin is administered—you'll be much more comfortable there, I promise, and the paediatric consultant is a very nice man.'

Hannah turned away to hide her wry smile. Once again the ladykiller smile had done its job and the poor woman was like putty in his hands.

For a few minutes the room was full of activity as Hannah took blood samples to send up to the lab for cross-matching purposes and Leo contacted Ross MacFadden to tell him what was on the way.

Hannah breathed a sigh of relief when the little family were finally on their way up to the ward, taking one lingering look at Leo's broad back as he followed them out of the room before she turned to the job of stripping the trolley and preparing it for the next patient.

At least their first meeting had gone off all right, she thought with relief as she finally allowed herself to think about it. They had both behaved as professionally as ever in spite of the explosion of passion they had shared last night.

How much of that was due to the fact that

they had both been occupied by a sick child and a couple of worried parents she didn't know, but if there was some way of making certain that they were always surrounded by other people then he wouldn't have a chance of saying anything personal to her.

Now all she had to do was stay out of his way until. . .

'Alone at last, you gorgeous creature!' growled a voice behind her just before her shoulders were seized and she was drawn around and tilted back over a muscular arm in a dramatic parody of a silent-screen kiss.

'L-Leo. . .!' she squeaked breathlessly, but there was no time to say any more as his lips met hers and stole her breath away completely.

At first her hands clutched at the lapels of his white coat as she tried to keep her balance, but when the tip of his tongue demanded entry and effortlessly recreated the same passionate onslaught of the night before she realised with the tiny corner of her mind which was still functioning that her arms had crept up to twine their way around his neck in surrender.

Dimly she became aware of a high-pitched bleeping and she'd begun to wonder vaguely whether it was a warning that her pulse rate had just exceeded safe levels when Leo dragged his mouth away from hers with a groan.

'Damn pager,' he muttered as he straightened up.

His gaze was fixed fiercely on her face, flicking from her kiss-swollen lips to her desire-drowsy eyes, as his hands sensuously massaged the curves of her shoulders as though he couldn't bear to let go of her.

It took several seconds before she could focus properly and realised the significance of what she was seeing.

She felt an extra twist of arousal deep inside when she realised that he was every bit as reluctant to part from her to answer the summons as she was to let him go.

'Stirling,' he growled when he reached out and grabbed the phone, and she was certain that the number had been tapped out by luck more than careful attention.

Hannah started to come to her senses while she watched his frown of concentration and realised that he still had one arm wrapped firmly around her shoulders, as though he was intending to continue where he'd left off when his pager had interrupted them.

Part of her would like nothing better than to

do just that, but the sane, sensible person that she'd had to become over the last two years knew that there was no point in allowing it to happen.

Subduing a pang of regret for yet another set of might-have-beens, she slid out from under his arm and managed to evade his distracted attempt at recapture to put herself out of his reach.

She hadn't realised exactly how wobbly her knees were until she tried to walk out of the room, but if she didn't put some distance between them before his call ended there was every chance that he would take it as an invitation to continue, and she was honest enough to admit—to herself at least—that she didn't think she'd find the strength to drag herself away from his arms again.

'Hey. . .! Hannah. . .!' she heard him call as the door swung shut behind her, and she took off up the corridor like a scared rabbit.

She had a terrible feeling that she couldn't afford to let him catch up with her before she'd regained her equilibrium or she'd be falling into his arms like a ripe plum—again!

CHAPTER EIGHT

'DIABETIC collapse on the way in,' Polly called as she put the phone down. 'ETA four minutes.'

Hannah raised a hand in acknowledgement and reached for a fresh set of gloves, pulling them on as she set off towards the doors.

It was her turn again to act as reception committee as the ambulance arrived, and she wasn't looking forward to it—the weather had turned decidedly cold today, and unfortunately the emergency entrance was situated on one of the bleaker sides of the building.

Oh, the architects had thoughtfully provided the area with a canopy so that staff and patients were sheltered from the worst of the weather, but it was still horribly draughty.

At least the ambulance was nearly here so she shouldn't have to wait long. . .

There was the distant sound of one of the new-style sirens and she wrapped her arms around herself and stepped outside. . . But suddenly she couldn't hear it any more and shook her head in confusion as she glanced down at her watch. The ETA was down to two minutes so she *should* be able to hear it by now. . .

Another ten minutes of waiting and shivering passed and she was just beginning to wonder if the call had been a hoax after all when she heard the siren's unmistakable new *'wa-wa-wa-shh'* sound again.

'What kept you?' she chided Ted as she rubbed her hands up and down her arms and danced from one foot to the other. 'It's far too cold at this time of year to get stood up!'

'We picked up an extra passenger,' he said as he backed expertly down the steps, without having to look to see where he was going. 'Someone stepped out in front of us on the way in.'

'What?' Hannah gasped. 'You didn't hit them, did you?'

'No, no. . . They were flagging us down for their friend who'd just hit his head. . .'

He paused as he grabbed his clipboard and the whole cortège moved swiftly into the warmth of the building.

'Who have we got here?' demanded Leo as he met them in the emergency room, and Ted correctly took it for an invitation to start his report.

'This is David Lyall. He's a twenty-year-old who's been a diabetic for three years. He was studying late last night and forgot to set his alarm to wake him up in time to have breakfast this morning. Collapsed running for a bus. When we got to him he was staring vacantly into space and his skin was cold and clammy. Rapid pulse—one-twenty plus—dilated pupils and muscle tremors.'

While Ted was speaking Leo's hands were competently making their own assessment, but it didn't stop him from paying close attention to Ted's words.

'We gave him oxygen while we checked his blood-sugar level and it was almost too low to read so I gave him a glucagon injection to keep him going while we brought him in—didn't want him going into a coma on us.'

'Well, he's certainly coming out of it better than he might have done,' Leo muttered, and Hannah knew what he meant. It had only been a week or so ago that they'd had another young diabetic collapse in an almost identical way, mistakenly hoping that as long as he took his insulin on schedule he could catch up on his meal when her had time.

Unfortunately, *he'd* gone into cardiac arrest

before anything could be done for him.

In David's case, the energy he'd used running for his bus had probably been the final straw which had flipped his system into hypoglycaemia.

If his friends had hesitated about calling for an ambulance when he'd collapsed, or if Ted's crew hadn't been free to race to his help, they could have been entering the details of another pointless waste of a young life.

She saw the notation Leo put on David Lyall's file and smiled wryly. He would be receiving a visit from the diabetes counsellor before he was released from the hospital to remind him—if today's scare hadn't been enough—that he couldn't afford to mess about with his routine, even if late-night studying for his exams was essential. The type of insulin he was on didn't give him the same warning he'd have got on the older type.

'And I suppose this is your hitch-hiker?' Leo enquired as he turned towards the second trolley, leaving Hannah to finish the setting-up of the second slow administration of dextrose through the wide-bore IV.

He was going to have to wait until his levels

were testing normal before he was set loose on the world again.

'Doctor?' David Lyall interrupted, the panic in his shaky voice drawing Leo back to face him again. 'What about my exams? I'm supposed to have been starting one at half past nine this morning and I've got another one this afternoon, and if I don't attend I'll automatically fail and then my grant might be cut off and—'

'Whoa! Calm down, calm down,' Leo ordered as he waved a placating hand at his agitated patient. 'Don't get yourself in such a state. I can write you a certificate to present to your college principal—it's not as if you've been swinging the lead this morning. At least that should give you a chance for a resit exam if they can't let you through on your coursework so far.'

The young man subsided with a heartfelt, 'Thanks, Doctor,' and submitted with rather more equanimity to Hannah's attentions.

'Sorry about that,' she heard Leo say as he returned to his second patient. 'Now, what have *you* been up to?'

Hannah hadn't had more than a glance at the young man on the other trolley and had only seen the fact that he had a large handful of blood-soaked dressing held against his head.

'This is Steve Wright,' Ted began when it seemed that the patient wasn't up to answering for himself. 'He's a nineteen-year-old trainee carpenter, working on one of the houses damaged by the gas blast the other week. According to his workmate—the one who flagged us down—he was doing a repair on a sash window when the thing came adrift and fell on his head.'

'Did he lose consciousness?' Leo asked as he tested the young man's ocular reflexes with his penlight.

'Knocked him out cold for a good five minutes, apparently. His friend had helped him out of the house to get some help but he was staggering around and was still pretty groggy when we picked him up. He knows his name but doesn't seem to be quite with it.' Ted shrugged. 'We put the neck collar on him as a precaution, even though he was already on his feet.'

'In that case. . .' Leo began, then paused. Out of the corner of her eye Hannah saw him frown as he tested the young man's eyes again. He was obviously concerned about something.

'Right, Ted,' he said decisively. 'You might as well get back to your trusty chariot. Thanks for these two. . .'

Ted acknowledged his appreciation for Leo's thanks with a brief wave and, collecting up his own equipment, left them to it.

'How are you doing over there?' Leo murmured as the X-ray technician bustled about, setting things up.

She'd seen him straighten up from his inspection of the damage under the dressing and scrawl something on Steve's notes, his bold slashing writing achingly familiar to Hannah.

'Oh, Mr Lyall and I have got to the boring bit now,' Hannah said from the other side of the room, smiling to cover up the fact that watching Leo work was turning into a refined sort of torture while her heart was still aching with all the things she couldn't have. 'We've just got to keep an eye on the readings at intervals until we can get the insulin and sugar properly balanced.'

'In which case, as soon as we get the all-clear from Mr Wright's neck X-ray you could lend me a hand here while I sew him back together. The quicker we get it done the better job it'll be.' He paused for a moment in thought, the top of his pen tapping idly against his chin.

'Then,' he continued suddenly, as though there had been no break in the conversation, 'I'll have to see if I can find him a bed for a while so that someone can keep an eye on him.'

'Ocular reflexes?' Hannah said questioningly, wondering how badly concussed their patient was if Leo was intent on admitting him. Had something about the way his pupils had reacted to light given him cause to be worried that there might even be hidden damage inside the young man's skull?

Leo gave a slight grimace, showing that she'd rightly guessed at his concern, and then, as the X-ray results were given the thumbs-up, he beckoned her to come closer.

Hannah resigned herself to another half-hour of intimate contact with the only man who raised her pulse level. Every time she had to hand him anything, or their bodies brushed each other, she would be reminded by a surge of that strange electricity which seemed to pass between them that they had been so much closer than this last night—more abandoned and somehow very much more intimate than she'd ever been with any other man. . .

'It's a shame the wound is too extensive for

us to superglue it together,' he murmured as they waited for the local anaesthetic to take effect, and Hannah murmured her agreement as he concentrated on clearing the field of operations by clipping the hair back along the edges of the wound.

She watched with approval as he took the time to make a good job of neatening up the ragged edges of the torn skin to achieve better approximation. She knew only too well how much difference the care taken at this stage could make to the appearance of the finished scar—and if the young man was lucky enough to avoid going bald this scar might even spend most of its time completely hidden under his thick thatch of hair.

'I'm going to need five-oh monofilament for this, and if all goes well they'll be able to come out in five days,' Leo muttered, half his words directed at her and half at the young man under his hands.

He might as well not have bothered for all the interest his patient was taking, his expression as blank as if it were all happening to someone else.

Hannah retrieved the necessary supplies and acted as handmaiden as she watched Leo tie a neat row of stitches along the length of the wound, knowing that he'd chosen to use non-dissolving ones to make certain that the edges couldn't accidentally be released too soon.

As the whole process continued she grew more and more concerned that their patient did little more than grunt in answer to their attempts at conversation and was finally forced to say as much to Leo.

'Do you think he's usually this taciturn, or could it be a result of the blow to his head?' she asked quietly.

'Could be either—he took a heck of a crack to make this sort of mess of himself. At a guess, he must have the mother and father of all head-aches and doesn't feel much like socialising.'

In spite of Leo's rational explanation, Hannah felt the worried frown pleating her forehead as she kept an eye on their taciturn patient. . . She had the strange feeling that there was another explanation.

'Right, old man, that'll do for you,' Leo announced cheerfully as he snipped the tail of the last stitch and dropped everything into the bowl Hannah held towards him, dragging his disposable mask down to dangle around his neck. 'Now, I'll just see whether I can arrange a bed somewhere. . .'

Hannah happened to be watching the young man's face as Leo continued speaking, and noticed that for the first time he seemed to be concentrating properly, a grimace tightening his lips when Leo mentioned arranging for him to stay in hospital.

A glimmer of an idea came to her and she pulled her own mask down before she spoke.

'How long do you think he'll have to stay in hospital?' she asked as Leo stripped off his gloves and automatically disposed of them as he strode across the room.

He paused with one broad shoulder against the door, ready to push it open, his puzzled expression probably the result of her unusually deliberate way of speaking.

As she'd hoped, their young patient's eyes had flicked across to Leo, as if he was waiting for him to answer, his eyes fixed intently on his face.

'If there are no complications he'll probably go home tomorrow—tonight, even, if there's someone responsible who can keep an eye on him at home.'

'Yes-s,' hissed their young patient hoarsely,

and Hannah saw Leo's startled blink of surprise.

'Ah, you're with us again, are you?' Leo asked as he came back across the room.

Hannah touched the young man's hand to draw his attention before she began speaking.

'I don't think he ever left us,' she said slowly and clearly, making sure their young patient could see her face while she was speaking. 'I think he needed to be able to *see* us talking to read our lips, and he couldn't when we were wearing masks.' She flicked the offending object hanging around her neck.

'Yes-s,' Steve repeated with a wry smile, an intelligent gleam in his eyes as he pointed to his ear. 'Hearing not good. . . Lost hearing aid. . . Headache bad. . . Hard to concentrate.'

'In which case, I apologise,' Leo said with a smile of his own and the offer of his hand. 'If I'd only realised, I would have made sure I explained what was going on before we did it. It must have been very confusing for you.'

He paused for a minute in thought.

'When you said yes, did you mean that there's someone at home who can keep an eye on you?'

'Yes-s. My mum,' he said succinctly, and

fumbled for his trouser pocket to draw out a wallet. 'On the telephone,' he continued in his strangely monotonous voice, pulling out a piece of paper with an address and telephone number clearly printed out. 'She worries about me,' he added with a typical male grimace.

'Well, that shouldn't take long to arrange,' Leo said with an easy smile then paused again, before adding cautiously, 'It was a nasty knock so I'd still like you to stay with us until this evening but then, if everything's OK, you can go home.'

'OK,' he agreed with a more cheerful thumbs-up and settled his head gingerly back against the pillow as Leo turned and strode out of the room.

Hannah drew in a deep breath, feeling as if there was suddenly so much more air to breathe in the room now that his larger-than-life presence was out of the way.

She quickly disposed of the soiled swabs and dressings, replenished the trolley and set it to rights, before pushing it neatly out of the way against one wall, then ran the next check on David's insulin and sugar levels.

She'd hardly completed that task when Leo breezed back into the room with Tina Wadland

and a wheelchair-pushing porter in tow.

'All arranged,' he said as he scanned Steve Wright's notes and initialled them before he turned and spoke directly to their young patient. 'You're being admitted upstairs for observation until we're certain you're not going to keel over on us.'

'OK, Doctor,' he said. 'Head too bad to argue.'

Leo chuckled. 'The painkillers should take that away soon,' he promised before he turned towards the room's other occupant.

'In the meantime, Nurse Wadland is going to check Mr Lyall's sugar levels and keep him company to make certain he behaves himself.'

He winked at the young man who had definitely improved enough to be showing signs of interest in the pretty nurse walking towards him.

'Now, Sister.' Leo turned his attention on Hannah and her heart gave a sudden thump before she firmly got herself under control.

'If I could have your assistance. . .?' he continued as he led the way briskly out of the room, and Hannah had no option but to follow him, expecting that he was leading her into one of the other treatment rooms to help him with the next patient.

Instead he continued to stride away down the corridor, and she almost had to run to keep up with his long-legged stride.

'Leo... Dr Stirling?' she called, suddenly mindful of hospital etiquette. 'Where are we going?' she demanded breathlessly when she finally caught up with him just as he pushed open the door leading to the emergency stairwell.

'Out here,' he said as he gently grasped her elbow to pull her through the door after him, 'in the vain hope that no one will think of looking for us until we've had five minutes alone.'

His words were so unexpected that it took Hannah several seconds to understand what he'd said, then her heart clenched tightly in her chest with foreboding, her elbow still feeling the heat of his hand even though he'd now released her.

She'd honestly thought that as long as she kept calm and made certain that there was always someone else in the room with her Leo wouldn't bother forcing this confrontation—she'd even hoped that he might eventually forget all about the unfortunate episode last night. . .

She should have known better.

He might have seemed perfectly calm as they were treating patients just a few minutes ago, but now that they were alone he seemed filled with an almost feverish intensity as he turned to face her, his hands clenching and unclenching as though he needed some physical activity to disperse the tension inside him.

Hannah drew in a deep breath and released it slowly while she collected her scattered thoughts, but when she realised that his gleaming eyes were quietly cataloging her every movement and expression she felt her shoulders stiffen with renewed determination.

She had made her decision, she reminded herself silently, conscious that her chin had come up a belligerent notch.

It didn't matter that she had fallen in love with him—she knew that Leo would never. . . *could* never. . .fall in love with her in return.

His confession about the pain of losing his fiancée to leukaemia had only reinforced her view of him as a confirmed bachelor so she would just have to cope with her unwanted feelings on her own.

The way she always had. . .

While she waited for him to start the conversation the little voice inside her head insisted that she remembered that she was no milk-and-water wimp to be intimidated into doing or saying anything she didn't want to. She was, after all, a responsible mature adult who had made a calm logical decision about her life.

She had no reason to explain any more than she wanted to and, knowing who and what he was, she certainly had no need to fear that Leo might try to force her to change her mind.

'Well?' he said, the word a mixture of boyish eagerness and impatient demand, as if he'd actually been waiting for *her* to start the ball rolling.

His voice sounded deeper and huskier in their echoing surroundings and she was almost overwhelmed by the feeling that he was having difficulty holding himself in check.

'Well, what?' she returned blankly, not certain what he was asking.

Her own voice sounded infinitely less substantial than his, almost thready as it hovered between them in spite of the fact that she'd tried to make herself sound calm and in control.

For just a second she thought she saw an

expression of hurt cross Leo's face, but it was gone so quickly that she couldn't be sure.

He distracted her by taking a step backwards to lounge back easily against the fireproof door, crossing his ankles and hooking his thumbs casually in his trouser pockets.

Suddenly she realised that, intentionally or not, he had positioned himself so that the only way she could avoid this conversation with him was to climb up the echoing stairs to the next floor or brave the bitter weather outside.

'Suppose we start with the basics,' he said heavily, all the eagerness gone from his voice. 'I'll ask you how you are and you'll answer.'

'I'm fine, thank you,' Hannah replied, wondering exactly where this strange conversation was going to end up.

'Are you really?' Leo asked, abandoning his exasperated tone for one filled with concern, his eyes darkly intent on her. 'You almost seemed to pass out on me. . .afterwards.'

The hint of embarrassed colour along the high curve of his cheek-bones made her feel even more guilty about her pretence.

'I—It was late. . . I was. . .exhausted. . . The day. . .it was exhausting. . .' She stumbled to a halt in confusion when she saw the wicked grin start to creep up over his face.

'Oh, but worth every second,' he said, his husky voice sounding like a vow. 'Personally, I wouldn't mind exhausting you like that on a regular basis—who knows, sometimes you might even be able to stay awake long enough to kiss me goodnight?'

'No!' she gasped, horrified that he'd totally misunderstood what she'd been trying to say. 'I didn't mean *that*! I meant. . . I meant that I was tired after all the stress. . .the stress at work. . .the suicide. . .and. . .and then you gave me a hug and. . .and then we. . .but it didn't mean that we. . .it didn't *mean* anything. . .!'

Her impassioned words sounded like a frantic plea as they echoed around the bare stairwell and she was vaguely aware that she was wringing her hands together in her agitation.

Surely he didn't think that the two of them were ready to embark on some sort of red-hot liaison, just on the strength of one misguided encounter—no matter how mind-blowing it had been for her.

A bachelor like Leo, with his brand of stunning good looks and ladykiller smiles, had beautiful women queueing up for miles waiting for a chance to go out with him. He might be ready to think about entering a relationship now, but why on earth would he want to limit himself to her?

'Didn't *mean* anything?' Leo repeated heatedly as he straightened abruptly away from the door, scowling as he ploughed the fingers of one hand through his hair to leave it standing up in disarray. 'We made love for the first time last night and you didn't think it *meant* anything?'

'Well. . .' Hannah blinked in surprise. She hadn't expected him to react like this. He sounded. . .angry. . .? Hurt. . .?

She'd thought that by downplaying the significance of the event she would be be telling him what he wanted to hear—after all, it had been three years since he'd lost Lisa and he'd now reached his early thirties without looking for a permanent relationship. Had she been wrong in assuming that he didn't have any intention of settling down?

'Well, what?' he demanded.

'Well. . .I didn't think it would mean anything to someone like you,' she began tentatively, trying to feel her way through the minefield she seemed to have landed in.

'Someone like me,' he repeated ominously.

'What exactly do you mean by someone like me?'

Obviously, her choice of words had done nothing to defuse the bomb.

'S-someone footloose and fancy-free, a. . . an eligible bachelor with women running after him for. . .for his good looks and personality. . .'

She ground to a halt, closing her eyes tightly with embarrassment when she heard the echoes of her babbling words.

There was a long silence and she didn't dare to look at him, opting instead to wait in silence for the explosion.

Only it never came.

Instead, she heard the first rumbles of a deep chuckle, fighting its way up from the depths of his chest.

'So you think I have personality and good looks?' he questioned and chuckled again, the sound strangely smug as it wrapped itself around her and heated her cheeks.

Her eyes popped open and she saw that he was leaning back against the door again, and his grin was equally as smug as his voice.

'Well, of course you're good-looking,' she snapped with the impatience of embarrassment.

'You know that—you only have to look in the mirror to see it.'

'But I didn't know that *you* had noticed,' he murmured huskily, his eyes gleaming wickedly at her again. 'In all the time we've been working together you've paid me no more attention than. . .than a stack of bed-pans—perfectly functional but not in the least interesting if you're looking for a hug.'

'Bed-pans?' Hannah choked, and couldn't help the spurt of laughter which escaped her control. 'Leo, you're crazy!'

'Crazy enough to make you laugh,' he pointed out with a return to smugness.

'Oh, Leo,' she sighed, realising uneasily that he was right—he did seem to have the knack for cheering her up and. . .

'So, when can I take you out?' he asked, his soft-voiced question breaking into her wistful thoughts.

'Take me out?' she said with a frown.

'Yes, take you out,' he said encouragingly with a boyish grin. 'You know how it works. . . We find out which evening we're both off duty, and then we arrange to go out somewhere together or stay in together. . .' He allowed the husky words to die away suggestively as his heated gaze slid over her face and started its incendiary journey down her body.

Her own eyes started a similar journey from the tawny gleam of his hair across the width of his broad shoulders and down the long lean length of his body.

Her heart began to beat out a rapid tattoo against her ribs and her memory supplied the X-rated pictures for what had happened the last time the two of them had been alone.

If she agreed to go out with him she knew what would happen, knew how they would both want the evening to end—except that *this* time he wouldn't be satisfied with a repeat of their frantic mating against her front door but would want to take her to bed and undress her, and then. . .

She shuddered as she imagined the way that scene would end and shook her head.

'No, Leo. I can't,' she said softly, hoping her shaky voice didn't reveal just how much she wanted to agree. 'It. . .it wouldn't work.'

'Why not?' he shot back. 'We work well together in the department, and we get on well outside work—very well,' he added huskily as he straightened away from the door and prowled silently towards her.

'But what about afterwards?' she demanded as she took a nervous step backwards to try to avoid contact with his reaching hand.

'Afterwards?' he repeated in a preoccupied way as he ran the tips of his fingers down the skin of her inner arm and sent a shudder of awareness right through her. 'What do you mean—afterwards?'

'When you finish going out with me and start on your next conquest,' she elaborated stiffly as she folded her arms to keep them away from him. She couldn't concentrate properly when he was touching her.

'Have you thought how awkward it would be for both of us?' she continued hurriedly when he would have broken in. 'It would be far worse than the situation with Sexy Samantha—at least she works in another department on another floor. Can you imagine what it would be like for the two of us to try to work together when the relationship ended?'

Leo was silent for a moment, as though he was thinking carefully about her point of view, and she started to breathe more easily at the thought that she'd managed to avert a potential disaster.

'But what if the relationship didn't end?' he

suggested seriously. 'It doesn't have to, you know.'

Hannah gasped and the world stopped spinning for an eon as shock rocked her to her core.

'Don't. . .don't be silly,' she spluttered breathlessly when her lungs began to function again. 'Th—the hospital grapevine has been keeping count ever since you started working here, and you've never gone out with *any* of your dates more than a handful of times.'

'And I've never made love with any of them either,' he whispered as he caught her fluttering fingers and drew them up to the soft warmth of his lips.

'N-never. . .?' She felt her eyes widen as she gazed up at him in renewed shock.

'Never wanted to,' he added slightly awkwardly as a wash of colour crept up his face.

'But last night you. . .we. . .'

Hannah was speechless with the unexpected confession, her brain whirling as she tried to understand the new implications of what had happened between them the night before.

What *did* it mean?

What was he trying to tell her?

'Do. . .do you mean you've been impotent?' she suggested hesitantly, wondering if that was why he wanted to go out with her again. If his condition had corrected itself then that would explain why he wanted to. . .

'Good God, no!' he exclaimed with a mixture of horror and laughter. 'Far from it!'

'Then. . .then why?'

'You mean, apart from the fact that promiscuity is a very risky option these days?'

She nodded, suddenly conscious that he was still holding her hand when he brought it up to his lips for another kiss, then followed up with a gentle nibble on her knuckles and a soothing glide of his tongue which sent goose bumps right up her arm.

'Perhaps it's because I was waiting for someone special enough to come along,' he suggested softly as his warm breath bathed her hand. 'Someone who would make me want to throw away restraint in a glorious explosion of passion.'

Hannah drew in a startled breath as her body tightened deep inside in reaction to his graphic words, then firmly brought her emotions back under control.

'All very poetic,' she commented wryly, 'except that we've been working together for two years so why me and why now?'

'Perhaps it's because you've only just noticed me,' he suggested, just as his dreaded pager burst into manic life.

'Just noticed you!' she scoffed with a burst of startled laughter, and she snatched her hand away. Before he could think about blocking her access to the door she stepped around him and opened it. 'Pull the other leg—it's got bells on!'

CHAPTER NINE

OVER the last few years, Hannah had found that she didn't enjoy Christmas very much any more—it was such an essentially family time and she didn't have any family to share it with.

It seemed as if it was going to be particularly empty this year, especially as Laura and Polly were totally wrapped up in their new relationships.

Hannah had felt very noble when she'd volunteered for the lion's share of the holiday shifts to allow her friends to spend time with their loved ones, but she hadn't realised that Leo had decided to do the same thing or she might not have accepted their thanks so blithely.

'The trouble is that I don't know whether to keep my fingers crossed that we're quiet— when Leo will have plenty of time to torment the life out of me—or hope we're frantically busy—when he'll probably manage to make certain that we're all but laminated together at the hip!' she complained to her two friends when she found out what had happened to the rosters.

Polly and Laura laughed at her disgruntled expression.

'Of course, there *is* one other thing you'll have to worry about,' Wolff suggested as he came in on the end of the discussion.

'Oh, no,' Hannah groaned. 'What?'

'A revenge attack from Sexy Samantha?' he suggested. 'She won't be very happy that you're getting to spend so much time with the object of her relentless quest.'

'As if she'd see *me* as any sort of competition,' Hannah scoffed with a hidden pang for the painful truth. 'She must be the most beautiful woman on the staff, and I've never seen her with a single hair out of place.'

'She is rather stunning,' Wolff agreed, then yelped as Laura dug her elbow in his ribs before he continued thoughtfully, 'I must admit, though, I sometimes think it's only a matter of time before Leo succumbs to her charms.'

'Before Leo succumbs to *whose* charms?' demanded the man in question as he strode cheerfully into the room, his eyes zeroing in on Hannah as if she were the only one in the room.

His dark gold hair gleamed with jewelled fire as he prowled towards her past the string of Christmas decorations which someone had strung around the top of the cupboards, the colours rivalling his gaudiest tie yet.

'If you're talking about Hannah here. . .' He dropped an unanticipated arm around her shoulders and pulled her close enough to the lean length of his body to press a brief kiss on her tumble of dark curls before he released her, startled and breathless.

'I'm ready to succumb to her charms the moment she crooks her little finger at me, and I've told her so!' he declared boldly.

He winked broadly as if the whole idea was a joke and the rest of the group joined in the laughter.

Only Hannah knew how hollow hers sounded.

'Are you counting on the principle of third time lucky, Leo?' demanded Wolff as he lifted Laura out of her chair and settled her on his lap. He curved his arms tightly around her as if he couldn't have her close enough, then continued speaking.

'You missed out the first time when Polly chose her Prince. . .'

'And I got the Big Bad Wolff,' Laura butted in with an impish grin at the man wrapped around her, tilting her head back to deliver a noisy kiss on his cheek.

'So you think I'm after Hannah to make it third time lucky?' Leo sounded bemused at the idea, his eyebrow cocked up towards Hannah as if he was daring her to comment.

'Well, if we're sticking to fairy-tales and wise sayings,' she mused aloud, 'he might be unlucky enough to find out that there's only Beauty and the Beast left.'

'Hey! Be careful of my ego!' Leo objected, but his exclamation was drowned out by the chorus of laughter.

As she looked back, Hannah realised that at least that light-hearted conversation had helped to set the tone of the rest of the holiday period, with various members of the accident and emergency staff taking Hannah's side when Leo's pranks and innuendos began to get out of hand.

It had started with the mistletoe.

Just one little sprig of green with two translucent berries, but as fast as one member of staff spotted its resting place and warned her so Leo would move it to another location and catch her unawares, his sexy mouth swooping down to deliver yet another earth-shattering kiss.

It wouldn't have been so bad if she hadn't wanted his kisses so much. As it was, each new episode left her lips tingling and her body trembling with renewed desire.

Dammit, she was in love with the man and all he was doing was taunting her with something she could never have.

It was almost a relief when the department received a warning that a bottle-fight had broken out between rival gangs in the centre of town at the height of the New Year revelries leading up to the striking of midnight.

Suddenly there was no time for kiss-chase games as the department was inundated with so many wounded that it began to look like a battleground.

Apart from a larger than usual number of drunks and several people who were suffering from shock and hysteria, there were at least fifteen serious injuries due to arrive, two with suspected fractured skulls.

Once again the department swung into action like the well-oiled machine it was, with the triage team sorting everyone as they arrived.

'Thank goodness we're still on holiday rosters,' mumbled Tina as she swiftly cleared the debris from the previous patient and set everything up ready for the next one.

The speed and confidence with which she could achieve the job spoke volumes about the way she'd progressed since she'd first joined the department just three months ago.

'That's a point,' Hannah agreed as she replenished the trolley. 'At least we know they won't have had to cancel any routine admissions or defer any cold surgery because so few are booked to come in during Christmas and New Year.'

They'd barely finished speaking when the doors swung open and a partially clothed young man was wheeled in, with blood pouring down his face and neck and congealing in his dreadlocked hair.

'I got bottled,' he announced in a drunken voice as he gazed blearily around at his strange surroundings, his clothes reeking of alcohol and urine. 'Some bugger 'it me 'ead wiv a bottle.'

'He refused to lie down,' muttered the porter as he delivered his passenger to the side of the trolley and set the brakes. 'It was as much as I could do to persuade him to use the wheelchair, even though he's none too steady on his legs.'

As he spoke their patient made an abortive attempt at getting out of the wheelchair and nearly ended up measuring his length on the floor.

'Gently does it,' Hannah soothed as she caught his elbow just in time and directed his lunge towards the freshly prepared trolley. 'I think you'll be more comfortable if you lie down on here.'

He swung his matted head towards her, one arm raised threateningly in her direction until he caught sight of her.

'Hey. . .! You're a good-lookin' bit,' he slurred with a drunken leer. 'Too bloody clean, but I c'n soon take care of that. . . Jus' climb up 'ere with me—I'll soon make yer sweat a bit. . .'

The rambling came to a sudden halt as he lost his battle with gravity and slumped onto his back with a profane groan.

'Are you all right?' Leo muttered in Hannah's ear, and she swung her head to look up into golden eyes full of concern.

'No problem,' she assured him. 'He's too drunk to do anything more than talk.'

'It's that sort of trash that makes me tempted to start stitching without an anaesthetic,' he growled, and she couldn't suppress an answering grin.

'Still,' he continued, 'we have to take our pleasures where we can find them, and one of mine will be getting rid of this disgusting bird's nest so we can repair the damage.'

He picked up several rancid ropes of blood-soaked hair and lifted them gently away from the young man's head while Hannah leant forward to sever them with a satisfying snip of very sharp scissors.

'He'll hardly know himself when he wakes up,' Tina commented a few minutes later when the shearing job was finished to reveal the full scale of the damage to the young man's scalp.

'He certainly won't *want* to know himself when he finds out about his hangover in the morning,' Leo commented wryly as he irrigated the deadened wound thoroughly, checking for any fugitive shards of glass, then prepared to begin the painstaking task of piecing together the multiple gashes in the young man's scalp.

'Still,' he commented a few moments later, 'he should be well used to the experience by now—I reckon this is at least the third time someone's practised their embroidery on him.'

To Tina's horror, he pointed out the tracery of previous injuries which ran across his head in several directions.

'You'd think he'd learn after the first time,' the young trainee commented with a pained expression on her face. 'Is it really worth the agony over and over again, just for the sake of a few drinks?'

'Ah, well, some people are very slow learners,' Leo said cryptically as his eyes gleamed tiger-bright at Hannah over the top of his mask, full of hidden messages. 'They have to keep repeating something until they finally get it right. Who knows, perhaps this will be third time lucky for this young man?'

Hannah had to turn away for a second, pretending to check the arrangement of the suture tray in an attempt to hide the heat washing over her cheeks.

Wretched man.

He must know what those strange golden eyes did to her equilibrium, and as for referring to the conversation about his apparent pursuit of her. . .

'Well, at least it gives me plenty of practice with my stitching,' Leo added philosophically, as if he'd been talking about their patient all the time, and he held out his hand for the first needle. 'Perhaps, when I've finished, I'll check up on the computer and see if the other stitches were done here, too—find out whose handiwork the rest are and see who did the neatest job. . .'

He bent his head over the brightly lit table, but before he concentrated on placing the first stitch he managed a surreptitious wink at Hannah and set her pulse racing all over again.

'What *is* going on between you two?' Laura demanded when the last of the roisterers had departed to continue their singing and shouting elsewhere, and the staff could afford to collapse for five minutes with welcome cups of coffee.

The final tally had included over a hundred stitches, two broken collarbones, numerous skinned knuckles and black eyes, a broken wrist and a hairline skull fracture, apart from a near-riot when the rival groups came face to face in the middle of the reception area.

Hospital security had welcomed the assistance of a small contingent from the local police station to sort that little lot out without any further bloodshed, but now that the cleaners had been through with their mops and buckets the department had finally returned to normal.

'Which two?' Hannah murmured as she leaned her head back into the corner of the squashy settee and groaned with relief as she slid her feet gratefully out of her shoes.

'You and Leo, of course,' Laura said impatiently, as though it should have been obvious.

'There's no "of course" about it,' Hannah said in a flat monotone, without even bothering to open her eyes. 'There's nothing going on between the two of us, other than a very long-running, very tiresome joke.'

There was a long silence and it sounded as if Laura had accepted her words until Hannah felt the cushions dip and realised that she was leaning closer.

'I don't believe you,' Laura murmured. 'Every time you see him, or his name is mentioned, you try to hide your reaction but you go all pink and flustered... And, as for him, he can't keep his eyes off you—if I wasn't crazy about Wolff I could feel quite jealous. But if it's still a big secret, and you don't want to tell me about it. . .'

It was the soft sound of hurt in her friend's

voice that made Hannah open her eyes.

'Laura. . .' Hannah began and then paused, not quite certain how to continue.

What *could* she say to her friend when she honestly didn't know what was going on?

'It's all right, Hannah, I understand,' Laura said hurriedly as she moved away from her friend and leant forward to reach for her coffee. 'I realise that our friendship is changing, especially now that I've got Wolff in my life, but I thought you would at least let *me* in on the secret.'

'But that's just the point!' Hannah exclaimed, then glanced around furtively and lowered her voice again. 'There isn't a secret to *tell* you, Laura. The whole thing is just one of Leo's many elaborate pursuits, and you've probably realised by now that he never chases anyone *too* hard in case he catches them.'

'Then there really isn't a secret romance going on between you?' Laura asked, the disappointment on her face almost comical, if Hannah had felt like laughing. 'Oh, Hannah, I was so hoping that you were going to be as happy as Wolff and I are.'

'But I *am* happy,' Hannah insisted. 'I've got my own home, a career I love with good prospects for promotion and a circle of caring friends—of course I'm happy.'

'But you're not content,' Laura said shrewdly, her dark green eyes full of sympathy. 'I can see it in your face—and in your eyes,' she added when Hannah would have disputed the fact. 'I can recognise the loneliness you feel inside because I used to see the same thing when I looked in my mirror.'

'Oh, Laura,' Hannah sighed, knowing she was conceding that her friend was right.

'So what's gone wrong?' she probed gently, careful to keep her voice low enough to deter eavesdroppers. '*Is* it a case of Leo chasing you without any intention of catching you while you wish he would?'

'If only it was,' Hannah said wearily, and rubbed both hands over her face. 'For some crazy reason, he seems to have got it into his head that the two of us would make a good couple and he won't let go of the idea.'

'Well, what's so wrong with that?' Laura demanded pertly. 'You're obviously just as crazy about him so what's stopping you?'

'I'm *not*!' Hannah objected with a knee-jerk reaction, but when she saw the open scepticism in her friend's raised eyebrow she subsided with lips pressed tightly together.

'You're right, dammit,' she muttered when Laura had allowed the silence to drag on for several tantalising minutes. 'For all the good it'll do me,' she added in a soft whisper as her heart swelled with familiar misery.

'But. . .I don't understand,' said Laura, her forehead creased in a frown. 'He's in hot pursuit and you're in love with him—so what's stopping the two of you? The electricity the two of you generate when you're near each other could set off a nuclear reactor!'

Hannah felt the surge of heat in her face as she remembered the explosion of passion she and Leo had set off in her flat, and could have died of embarrassment. Unfortunately, Laura was too close to miss the tell-tale signs.

'Oh-ho!' she chortled and rubbed her hands together gleefully. 'This looks promising! Tell me. . .tell me. . .'

Hannah closed her eyes and sighed.

'It was only the once,' she admitted.

'And. . .?' Laura prompted with a giggle. 'Did it blow your socks off?'

'Actually, no. It happened so fast we only got as far as removing the essentials.'

'Wow!' Laura breathed, her dark green eyes

gleaming. 'But if it was that good why haven't you scheduled a re-match?'

'Because that's as good as it can get,' Hannah said cryptically. 'If I gave in to him and let him get too close I'd be left with just the memories.'

'But that's all you've got now,' Laura pointed out with stubborn logic.

'Yes,' Hannah agreed. 'But at least they're all *good* memories, and if I said yes to making love again he would want to spend the night with me and then I would have to tell him. . . to show him. . .' She halted, unable to finish the sentence.

'Tell him what? Show him what?' Laura demanded, obviously totally puzzled by the turn of the conversation.

Hannah drew in a shuddering breath and forced herself to meet her friend's eyes.

'The. . .the scars,' she whispered as her own eyes brimmed with tears. 'He'd have to see the scars. . .'

Her eyes were still slightly red when she came back from her break, in spite of the cold water she'd splashed on her face.

Laura had offered her some make-up but her

skin tone was so much paler that it was no use, simply making Hannah look as if she'd seen a ghost.

Laura had escorted her to the nearest bath-room when she'd broken down, shielding her from curious eyes until their privacy was guaranteed.

It had taken her some time to tell her friend about everything that had happened since they'd worked together at their previous hospital—from her discovery that her mother's recently discovered cancer had metastasised, to her funeral just six weeks later, to the revelation that there was a strong genetic link between all the cancer deaths in her family which had left her without a single living relative.

The story had come out in a torrent as she put the whole horror into words for the first time.

'Oh, Hannah, I'm so sorry I wasn't there for you,' Laura said with an impulsive hug. 'But you've come through it so well—I can't believe you're so frightened of telling him. If anything, you're stronger than you were when we were training and you know that Leo's just a big pussycat, in spite of his name.'

'A very big, very sexy, very good-looking

pussycat who can have his pick of all the beautiful people in the hospital,' Hannah pointed out miserably. 'What on earth would he want with damaged goods?'

Inside her head she heard the echoes of her ex-fiancé's voice as he'd broken off their engagement, his words seared into her soul like a brand.

'You ought to carry some sort of declaration,' Jon had declared with a twist to his mouth. 'You know, like the ones manufacturers stamp on faulty goods when they're trying to sell them off cheaply—"Imperfect" or "Seconds". . .' He'd held his hands up as if he were outlining the words in bold type. 'Or how about "Returned to maker unopened— Unwanted gift"?'

Even those insults hadn't been enough for him. He hadn't been satisfied with pointing out how much the sight of her offended him—he'd had to go on and attack her whole sense of self-worth, fragile as it had been at the time.

'Still, never mind,' he'd said with a sneer as he pocketed the sapphire and diamond engagement ring he'd told her he'd chosen to match the sparkle in her dark blue eyes. 'I understand there are some sickos out there who like to get it on with disabled people such as amputees so, who knows, you may get lucky one of these days. . .?'

'You've got to go and see Leo,' Laura said fiercely, breaking into Hannah's bitter memories and dragging her back to the painful decision she was going to have to make. 'You've got to talk to him.'

'But. . .'

'Look,' she interrupted before Hannah could voice her reservations, 'it's taken you months to tell me what's been happening to you, and I'm only your friend. If you love Leo as much as I think you do surely he deserves your honesty, too?'

In her heart Hannah knew that she was right but the memory of Jon's rejection was still fresh and raw, like an open wound.

Her determination to keep the rest of the world at arm's length had been so strong that she hadn't allowed herself to realise that she was falling in love with Leo—until passion had exploded between them and opened her eyes.

The trouble was that it had taken her such a long time to admit that she loved Leo—it had probably been growing, unrecognised, from the first time she'd seen his handsome face and distantly admitted to his sex-appeal—and that now if he, too, rejected her she didn't think she would ever recover.

'But what if he doesn't—can't—?'

'Enough of the what if and maybe, Hannah!' Laura exclaimed forcefully. 'You're doing the same as I did, and it's tearing you apart all the while you're in love with him and wanting to be with him and not having the guts to talk to him to find out how he feels one way or the other.'

'Oh, Laura, it makes me feel better just to know that you went through something like this, too,' Hannah said as she returned her friend's hug. She was all too aware that just the thought of talking to Leo was making her quiver inside, but she knew that Laura was right.

'OK,' she said, and drew in a steadying breath. 'I'll collar him at the end of the shift and. . .and suggest he comes back to my place for coffee and a chat.'

'Make sure you do,' Laura warned with an admonishing finger. 'You've got big enough circles under your eyes to audition for a panda. It's about time you started smiling again.'

Hannah showed Laura that she'd crossed her

fingers for luck as they went back to work, and she hoped there wouldn't be too many patients in the hours before the end of her shift. There was no guarantee that she was going to be able to concentrate properly on what she was doing if she was trying to compose her invitation in her head.

'Leo, would you like some coffee?' she practised under her breath, then shook her head. That was no good—he'd probably think she was offering to make him one in the little kitchenette, and there was no way they could have their talk *there*.

'Leo, are you free this evening?' she tried next, and grimaced as she realised that the words could sound as if she was asking him out on a date—the rest of the department would love to hear that one.

'Leo, would you like to come home with me. . .for coffee?' Lord, this was getting worse by the minute. Now she sounded as if she was propositioning him.

'Leo, I need to talk to you. . .' No, that was no good because he would only ask her why and she didn't want to start explaining until they were a long way from any eavesdroppers. What she had to tell him was not something she wanted to have broadcast on the hospital grapevine.

'Leo, I need. . .'

'What?' a deep voice demanded behind her and Hannah nearly jumped out of her skin.

'Oh, Leo, there you are,' she squeaked breathlessly, while her brain refused to produce a single one of the sentences she'd been trying out and she was left gazing up at him in silence.

'Hannah?' he prompted patiently. 'You said you needed something?'

'Oh, did I? I mean, yes, I did. I needed. . .I needed. . .' She gulped and drew in a sharp breath before she began again. 'Oh, Lord, Leo, I've got to talk to you before I go completely out of my head.'

He was silent, and for a horrible moment she was afraid that he was going to refuse—until she saw the gentle smile start in his eyes.

'And about time, too,' he murmured in a husky voice. 'Just tell me where and when.'

In the end it had all been so ridiculously easy that she hadn't had time to sort out the practical details, and she looked at him blankly.

'At the risk of sounding trite—your place or mine?' he suggested with a hint of a chuckle.

'Yours. . .no, mine,' she decided—at least

she wouldn't have to drive away from him if everything went badly but, then, if it *did* go badly she'd probably have to move flats because the rooms would be full of the memories of. . .

'What time?' Leo asked, his tone telling her that it wasn't the first time of asking.

'Is seven-thirty all right?' she offered hesitantly.

He agreed easily and his smile was a warm benediction that spread hope through her body before he strode away down the corridor. And then, as her eyes lovingly followed him until he turned the corner, she could have kicked herself.

Seven-thirty was *hours* away—far too much time for her to get her nerves knotted with anticipation and dread. What on earth had made her suggest it? If she'd said six. . .

Celia MacDonald's precise Scots accent hailed her urgently, breaking into her mental self-castigation, and in an instant everything else was pushed to a back corner of her mind as she whirled and set off briskly.

'Ah, good, Hannah,' the senior sister said with a shadow of her former briskness as she beckoned her into her room. 'The police are bringing one of our nurses in. She's going to need your special touch—she's been raped.'

Hannah's heart clenched in her chest.

It didn't matter that she'd had special training for these cases or that she'd seen so many of them. The feeling never went away—an overpowering mixture of compassion and anger. Compassion for the victims of this particularly loathsome form of violence and anger that *any* man thought he could get away with it.

This time it would be even worse because the victim was one of their own—one of the extended 'family' of hospital employees.

The anger was under control at the moment, but by the time she'd finished the necessarily intimate job of examining the victim and taking samples for any possible court case she would have spent a long time with her patient and would probably have heard enough details about the attack to make her look nervously over her shoulder for weeks.

What she *did* know was that if she met the man who'd done this thing she'd probably be so incensed by then that she'd willingly castrate him on the spot—at least he wouldn't ever be able to rape again. . .

'Hello, Su, I'm Hannah,' she said gently as

she let herself into the room and closed the door quietly behind her.

The slender young woman had been leaning against the wall on the other side of the room, her straight dark hair a concealing waterfall around her face and shoulders as she huddled into herself with her arms wrapped protectively around her ribs.

At the sound of Hannah's voice she whirled to face her, and Hannah couldn't help gasping at the state of her face.

'Oh, Su, your poor face,' she murmured, and she took an involuntary step towards her before she got herself under control.

Su gazed at her out of a face that was hardly recognisable as human, both eyes already almost swollen shut and with bleeding cuts on her cheek-bone and lips. One side of her face was so raw that it looked as if she must have been dragged along the street.

'Have. . .?' Hannah had to stop and clear her throat, giving herself a stern reminder that the young woman needed her professional expertise as much as her sympathy.

'Have you been told what we need to do?' she asked gently. 'Did the police tell you what the routine is?'

Su shook her head briefly and a single tear slid out of one discoloured eye.

'They wanted me to see the police surgeon,' she whispered through puffy lips. 'I told them I'd rather come here.'

She drew in a shuddering breath and winced, tightening her arms protectively around her ribs.

'I—I know most of the staff on A and E— by sight at least—and I trust you to do what you have to. . .'

'OK.' Hannah nodded, accepting her unspoken trust. 'You know you're safe here so the first thing I need to do is take a medical history.'

'My details are all in the hospital computer—I'm Sister Su Yuen and I work up on the special care baby unit. I'm twenty-seven, s-single and. . .and. . .'

'Hey, Su, take it easy,' Hannah soothed as the young woman started to lose control. She longed to be able to offer her the physical comfort of a hug but knew it wasn't possible yet, the only option being to distract her. 'Will it help if you focus on answering straight questions?' she asked instead.

'O-OK.' She nodded jerkily. 'Fire away.'

'Good girl,' Hannah said, amazed by her strength of will. She wasn't certain that she'd be holding up this well if it had happened to her.

'You're doing well, Su,' she said encouragingly. 'Are these the clothes you were wearing when you were attacked?'

'Yes,' she whispered. 'T-the police picked me up in the street after. . .after it happened and I made them bring me here.'

'Good. So you haven't been to the toilet or had a wash?'

'No.' She closed her eyes on a single sob. 'I remembered that part of the lecture during our training. . .'

'Well, in that case, I'm going to put on protective clothing so that I can't contaminate any of the evidence, and then I'll help you to take your clothing off and seal it in bags to go for forensic examination.'

Limiting herself to questioning Su about her injuries, Hannah quickly but thoroughly noted down her observations about the state of her clothing and her physical and emotional state, very conscious that her notes would constitute a legal document in any court case.

Su had caught her hand in a death-like grip

when Nick Prince had come in to take swabs and make the necessary internal examination, and by the time she'd combed the poor woman's pubic hair for foreign samples, taken internal swabs and scraped under Su's fingernails for traces of her attacker's skin Hannah was feeling completely drained.

It seemed like hours before the young policewoman stepped in to take charge of the various items of evidence, her sympathetic smile apparently the last straw for the trauma-tised young woman.

'It's all a waste of time,' she wailed as she finally gave in to hysterical tears. 'They said the evidence won't do any good because there were too many of them. . . And. . .and they said they'd tell Mike I wanted them to do it. . .that I like a bit of rough stuff. . .'

The policewoman stopped in her tracks as if she'd hit a brick wall, her expression one of total horror.

'What?' Hannah whispered in disbelief as she closed her arms around the terrified young woman, who trembled against her like a wounded animal. 'Do you know who did this to you?'

CHAPTER TEN

'SOMETIMES I could willingly commit murder,' Hannah muttered as she coaxed her elderly car into life, her mind still consumed by the details Su Yuen had finally given the young policewoman.

The Mike that Su had mentioned was her fiancé, an orthopaedic registrar at St Augustine's who had raced to be with her as soon as he heard that Su had been hurt.

Amidst her entreaties that she should be allowed to tell Mike the details herself, she'd told the sympathetic officer that they'd only been engaged for a month and that her attackers today had been his team-mates from the local rugby club he'd joined shortly after he began his medical training. She'd only met them for the first time the previous week at their engagement party at her parents' Chinese restaurant.

'They got drunk at the party,' she'd told the two of them through her tears. 'In front of both of our families they told Mike he was making a mistake in wanting to marry me. That everyone knew Chinese women were the best whores in the world—trained to please from the cradle. . .'

When the young officer's questions had finished Hannah had pieced together a tale of Mike's disgust with his team-mates' behaviour and his decision to quit the club, in spite of his leading part in the team.

It seemed as if their attack on Su had been a particularly sick form of revenge when the team had lost an important game without Mike on their side, and in their drunkenness they had actually made themselves believe that once they had all used her Mike would dump her and rejoin the club.

It was just an added agony for the young woman that she'd been a virgin, determined to save herself for the man she loved on her wedding day.

She was late, but there was no way she could have left Su before she was certain that she had someone else there to care for her.

Mike had been pacing a furrow in the corridor outside and tears clogged Hannah's throat when she remembered the gentle care with which he'd wrapped his injured fiancée in his arms.

The clock on the dashboard showed that it was already seven-thirty by the time she drew up behind the other cars parked outside her flat, and she sighed tiredly.

Hannah was just thinking that the only good thing about the events of the last few hours was that they'd stopped her thinking about her own problems when she saw the door on the car immediately in front of her open, and Leo climbed out and straightened up.

'You're late getting back,' he commented as he came forward to relieve her of one of her bags. 'Big Mac told me what was going on. Does your invitation still stand or would you rather make it another day?'

The coward inside Hannah wanted to grab at the chance to postpone their discussion but she knew that she couldn't bear to wait any longer. She had to know whether there was a chance for the two of them to build some sort of relationship together, and the sooner she knew the better.

'No. This evening's fine, provided you're not expecting the place to be tidy.'

She had a vivid memory of how neat his

own flat had been when he'd taken her there to dry off—not at all the typical picture of a bachelor's domain.

'It *must* be better than mine,' he commented while he waited for her to find her key in the muddle at the bottom of her bag.

'Yours? You must be joking!' she exclaimed in surprise. 'I've only been there once and it was immaculate—quite put me to shame!'

'Ah, well, that must have been the day that Audrey was there,' he said with his familiar ladykiller grin.

Hannah bit her tongue to stop the jealous words escaping, but it was no use.

'Audrey?' she heard herself echo. 'Who's Audrey?'

'Audrey's a wonderful woman who comes every week to shovel up my mess and put me straight for another week—every bachelor should have an Audrey!'

'Not just bachelors,' Hannah said, glowering to hide her relief that the mystery woman in his life was his cleaner as she pushed the door open and carried her bag through to her tiny kitchen.

She grimaced at the neat pile of crockery and cutlery waiting in the sink. 'It would be wonderful to come home, knowing that a good fairy had come and washed up the breakfast things in my absence.'

'In which case, it's a good thing I had time to pick this up,' Leo said, holding up the carrier bag dangling from his other hand.

Suddenly Hannah's nose was assailed by the tempting smells of Chinese food, and her stomach rumbled loudly.

'I hope that's what I think it is,' she said fervently as she reached up into a cupboard for two plates. 'Do you want chopsticks or forks?'

'Chopsticks,' he voted with a grin. 'I like showing off!'

Hannah handed him a tray on which to set the foil containers, and while he carried them through and put them on the table she collected serving spoons and soy sauce and followed him through to sit on the other side of her tiny table.

After his implied boast, Hannah had been prepared for Leo to be a dab hand with chopsticks so it came as rather a surprise to find that he was dropping more than he managed to carry to his mouth.

'Leo!' she laughed when he lost control of yet another chunk of chicken and was left with his mouth open like a baby bird in a nest.

'You're going to starve at this rate!'

She reached out and neatly scissored her own chopsticks around a plump button mushroom and lifted it towards him.

'Here,' she offered. 'Open wide.'

Leo's eyes flared as he fixed them on her own and she suddenly realised how intimate a gesture she'd made when she watched his lips close over the smooth shape of the mushroom.

'Mmm,' he murmured as he made short work of the mouthful. 'More, please.'

Hannah hesitated, aware that her hand had started to tremble, but his eyes gleamed at her, daring her to feed him again.

'It's your turn this time,' she said, her voice huskier than usual. 'Turnabout's fair play.'

His eyes darkened as he accepted the challenge and suddenly he was able to manipulate the slender implements with no difficulty at all, tempting her with a succulent strip of chicken.

'You cheat!' she mumbled with her mouth full. 'You were only pretending you couldn't manage!'

'It worked, though, didn't it?' he teased gleefully, chuckling as he scooped up a goodly portion of fried rice and transferred it to his mouth without losing a single grain.

'But why the pretence?' she demanded as she fished for another sliver of chicken.

'Because I wanted an excuse to feed you,' he admitted simply, his laughter gone as he held out a perfect prawn and touched it to her lips. 'Open up,' he whispered, his eyes flicking from her mouth to her eyes and back again.

Suddenly Hannah was nervous of his intensity, and the tip of her tongue darted out to collect the moisture he'd left there.

'Oh, God, Hannah,' he groaned, and abandoned the chopsticks with a clatter. 'I can't think about eating when I see you licking your lips like that. All I can think about is kissing you and tasting the sweet and sour sauce on your tongue.'

He reached out to take her own chopsticks away, her hand frozen around them in spite of the fact that she'd completely forgotten they were there.

'Leo,' she heard herself whimper as he stood up and reached over to lift her from her own chair and enfold her in his arms.

'Kiss me, Hannah, please,' he whispered as he pulled her tightly against his body and angled his head towards her. 'I need you.'

His husky words caused a sharp twist of

desire deep inside her and she was helpless to refuse him, her head settling against his shoulder and her lips parting for him almost before his mouth touched hers.

It was like coming home.

Only with Leo did she have this sensation that she had found the place she belonged, and when his tongue took possession of her mouth she knew that her submission to his penetration was only the symbol of her willingness for a far deeper surrender.

Her head was swimming by the time he lifted her in his arms and cradled her against his chest.

'This time I refuse to rush anything,' he declared roughly as he set off across the room towards the door of her bedroom. 'This time I want us to be able to take our time and make love in comfort, and if you fall asleep on me again I want to be able to cuddle your naked body next to mine until you're ready to wake up and start all over again.'

As he spoke he was sliding her down his body so that her feet touched the floor and she was achingly aware of every virile inch of him.

His husky words should have been as exciting as the evidence that his tautly muscled body was already fully aroused and ready for love-making but on Hannah they had the same effect as a dousing with a bucket of icy water.

'No, Leo,' she gasped as panic overtook her and she tried to step back out of his arms. 'I can't. . . We can't. . . Not until. . .until. . . Oh, Leo, let me go. . .!'

He must have recognised the anguish in her voice because he released his hold on her so suddenly that she nearly fell over.

'Hannah?' He caught her elbow again and steadied her, a confused frown pleating his forehead when she froze in his grasp. 'Sweet-heart, what's the matter? What's wrong—don't you want to make love?'

'Oh, Leo. . .' Her throat closed when she saw the mixture of hurt and puzzlement in his eyes. 'Yes, I want to make love with you, but I can't—not until I've had a chance to tell you. . .to warn you. . .'

She shook her head. How was she ever going to find the words?

'Hey, sweetheart, whatever it is it can't be so bad,' he said supportively. 'If you want to talk to me then we'll talk, but we might as well make ourselves comfortable.'

Hannah felt for the edge of the bed behind

her shaky knees and sank gratefully onto it, lacing her fingers together into a Gordian knot as she tried to find the words to start.

'What's it all about?' he prompted as he sat himself beside her, gently lifting her white-knuckled hands into his own and smoothing their chill away with his own warmth.

'I—I suppose it's about my family, or rather my lack of one,' she finally began, deciding it was easier to start at the very beginning. 'Since my mother died just over two years ago there's only been me.'

'I'm sorry, sweetheart. And I can't offer you much more—just a set of parents I don't have time to visit very often.'

'How old is your mother?' she asked, and saw him blink at the apparent change of topic.

'She was fifty-seven this year. Why?'

'My mother was thirty-nine when she died. My aunt—her older sister—was forty-one and their mother was thirty-five.'

'Was there no one else?' He was still frowning as he tried to see which way the conversation was going.

'Just my cousin. She died when she was twenty-nine.'

'I take it from the tone of your voice that

there is some significance to all this?' His voice, too, was sombre and she knew his mind would be working with the speed of a high-powered computer as he tried to piece the picture together.

'All of them died of breast cancer,' she said bleakly. 'We're now one of the families that have been written up by researchers in the race to isolate and find a treatment for the breast cancer gene.'

'Have you been tested?' he asked, his tone as calm and even as if he were asking the time, every inch the professional doctor in spite of the fact that he was sitting beside her on the edge of her bed.

She nodded briefly.

'Just after Mum was diagnosed—too late for treatment—I caught part of a television pro-gramme about a woman who traced her family and found that a very high proportion of them had died of a particular type of breast cancer. As soon as I realised the significance of my own family history I asked if I could be tested, too.'

She gritted her teeth and started undressing herself, ignoring his startled glances as she first unclasped the ornate buckle she wore so proudly then started on the front fastening of the uniform she hadn't had time to change in her hurry to get home.

She forced herself to continue speaking, her voice trembling as much as her fingers as she relived the past and dreaded the future.

'At the same time as I was waiting for the chromatography results I also had a mammogram, and they found a small suspicious mass. It could have passed unnoticed if they hadn't been looking for it—but it was malignant.'

By this time she'd shrugged out of her dress and was reaching for the front fastening on her eminently practical bra.

'I had to make a decision,' she continued through a throat filled with tears as she forced herself to allow the bra to fall away from her body. 'The surgeon agreed that in view of my family history the only possible course of action was to take both breasts off.'

There was the brief sound of his sharply indrawn breath, and then silence.

Hannah closed her eyes, unable to bear to look at him—afraid what his expression would tell her.

'Ah, Hannah, love. . .' he murmured softly,

but she couldn't tell whether the tone was of pity or compassion.

She forced herself to open her eyes just in time to see his hand reach out towards the scars, and she flinched away from the contact.

'Still painful?' he asked.

'More emotional than physical,' she admitted as she fumbled awkwardly to settle the flesh-coloured prostheses in her bra and fasten it in position again.

'Was there some reason why you didn't undergo reconstruction immediately?' he demanded, and she smiled inwardly at the evidence that his medical brain was still functioning as usual.

'At the time I was so depressed with the combination of my mother's death and my own diagnosis—' *and Jon's hurtful derision*, her silent inner voice reminded her '—that I didn't see the point of having the implants done. It seemed like a waste of time when none of my relatives had survived more than a few months after diagnosis.'

'But that was more than two years ago and your prognosis is good—surely you've made fresh enquiries about having implants at one of your check-ups?'

'I manage,' she said woodenly. 'It seemed like an awful lot to go through just for the sake of vanity. . .another operation, more scarring, and they still wouldn't be real breasts. . .'

Distracted by her memory of Jon's derision at the pointlessness of her original intention to have implants—and his scorn that they might make her *look* normal to anyone else but he'd know better—she was struggling to pull her uniform up over her shoulders again and didn't realise that he'd reached out to help until he brushed her naked skin.

She froze like a small creature caught in the beam of a bright light, unable to move while he was touching her.

He started to lift his hand away and then grew still, his warm fingertips still in contact with her cooler flesh.

She could almost hear his brain working— hear him calculating and analysing, sifting the information she'd given him and reading between the lines for the things she *hadn't* said.

'Who was he?' Leo demanded suddenly with anger in his voice. 'Who's the bastard whose shoes you've got me wearing?'

He leapt to his feet and strode to the other end of the bed, then whirled back to face her.

'Who was the insensitive clod who tried to destroy your self-confidence at a time when he should have been supporting you?' he demanded, his eyes fiercely intent.

'J-Jon. . .my fiancé,' she confessed, unable to withstand the force of his glittering glare. 'H-he couldn't help. . . He couldn't look. . . T-the sight of the scars. . .' She shrugged helplessly.

She saw Leo's hands clench into fists and suddenly knew that he was imagining what he would like to do to Jon. . .

The thought that Leo wanted to punish Jon for his shabby treatment of her was like balm to her soul, but it didn't alter the fact that. . .

'And *that's* the reason why you wanted to invite me here,' he said suddenly as comprehension and icy anger clashed in his voice. 'I was starting to be a nuisance, chasing after you when you weren't interested in anything more than a one-night-stand, and you thought you'd hit on the perfect way to get me out of your hair.'

'No!' Hannah gasped, horrified that he could have misunderstood so completely. 'It was for *your* sake—so you wouldn't waste any more time on. . .on someone like me when there are so many beautiful women you could have been going out with. . .f-falling in love with. . .'

'Damn you, Hannah,' he said harshly, his face ashen. 'Do you think I'm *that* shallow? Do you think so little of me that you think I can't see past external appearances?'

'No, Leo! I only—'

'Dammit, woman, I'm in love with you,' he continued, totally ignoring her attempt at explaining. 'I've been in love with you ever since I met you and you'd never give me more than a vague smile. . . But I still hoped. . .'

'Leo. . .' She didn't know whether to laugh or cry. He *loved* her. . .

'As if it makes the slightest difference to me whether you've got breasts or not,' he exclaimed furiously. 'It. . .it's as if you fell in love with a man, then decided you couldn't love him any more if he lost a leg in a crash!'

He whirled away from her and strode out of the bedroom, and suddenly Hannah came out of her happy daze with the realisation that he wasn't coming back.

'Leo?' She scrambled to her feet and sped after him, arriving just in time to see him thrusting his arms into his padded jacket. 'Leo, you can't go yet!'

'There doesn't seem to be a great deal of point in staying,' he said curtly, hardly glancing in her direction.

'But. . .'

She drew in a shuddering breath.

How on earth could she get him to stay long enough for her to explain. . .?'

'You said you love me. . .' she began, holding on tightly to the miraculous revelation.

'For all the good it does me,' he growled, swinging to face her like an angry bear. 'You obviously don't love me in return or you'd never have believed that your sad little stripte-ase would have any effect on my feelings for you. What were you thinking? That all it would take was one look at you and you wouldn't see me for dust?'

'But I didn't know. . .' she began, then had to bite her lips when they quivered uncontrollably, tears horribly close when she realised how badly she'd misjudged him.

He squeezed his eyes tight shut and shook his head.

'I'm sorry,' he said on a deep sigh. 'Sorry that I put you through this. . .this. . .' He waved an expressive hand and shrugged. 'I'll see you at work and I promise not to embarrass you any more in front of the rest of the department.'

And before she could draw another breath he was gone.

'Good morning,' Leo said politely as she arrived for work, but his expressionless eyes struck Hannah like a blow.

It had been a week since he'd left her to her tears, the remains of their meal congealing on the plates as a mute reminder of how well the evening had started.

If only she'd spoken to him without resorting to the melodrama of showing him her mutilated body. . . If only she'd known that he loved her then everything would have been different.

Now he was so distant and so excruciatingly polite that sometimes she felt like screaming.

Her eyes followed his long-legged stride helplessly as he walked away from her towards the staffroom and another of the cups of lethally black coffee he'd started drinking.

Her heart clenched with despair.

She couldn't stand this much longer. She couldn't sleep, couldn't eat and her concentration was completely shot. If something didn't change soon they'd be coming for her with a strait-jacket.

She turned and had begun to walk towards the reception area when she came to a halt in the middle of the corridor.

'This is stupid,' she muttered as she whirled and set off briskly after him. 'He said he loves me, and I love him. For goodness' sake, we're two adults—we should be able to talk to each other. . .'

She paused by the door and peered in through the safety glass. If the room was crowded she'd have to try to catch him later, but if there was a chance of talking to him now she was certain she could explain how everything had got so muddled. . .

Her thoughts ground to a halt at the sight that met her eyes.

Leo was laughing, his solemn face wreathed once again in his familiar ladykiller smile as he leant forward to kiss. . . Sexy Samantha. . .

Hannah's eyes lingered for a moment on the other nurse's radiant face and voluptuous body and she felt her heart shatter inside her.

Leo might have vowed that her mastectomy didn't matter, but facts spoke for themselves when he replaced her so quickly with someone so spectacularly endowed.

Hannah straightened her shoulders and

turned swiftly away, hurrying back towards the duties which awaited her.

At least now that she knew Leo had replaced her she wouldn't have to worry that he was still hurt by what she'd done. Now she'd be able to return to her original determination to make a lifetime's career of her nursing.

'Hannah? Trauma team,' Ceila MacDonald called as she returned the phone to its cradle. 'Another one in the suicide pit.'

Hannah groaned and turned to make her way swiftly to the emergency room, already able to guess what she'd be facing at the end of a high-speed journey—someone was trapped in the 'suicide pit' under a train.

Her mind was full of the last horrendous episode when a child had slipped and fallen off the edge of the platform in his excitement at his first train journey.

'I hate these,' Nia Samea muttered as the two of them zipped themselves into their protective clothing. 'Apart from the fact that we can't get at them properly to help them, it's always so bitterly cold—even in summer.'

She slid quickly into the emergency vehicle and Hannah followed her, crowding closely against her to make room for the last member to climb in.

'Ready,' Leo's deep voice announced as he pulled the door closed, but she hadn't needed to hear him to know who was sitting beside her.

Everywhere they made contact she seemed to feel the heat radiating out of his body, a strange sort of electricity which had never happened with anyone else and probably never would.

'Any details?' he demanded coolly, as if he hadn't even noticed who was sitting beside him.

'A jumper, apparently,' John Preece supplied from his seat beside the driver, using the common term for an attempted suicide. 'Whose turn is it to go under with him?'

'I'll go,' Leo offered, without the usual friendly banter about who'd done the dangerous, dirty job last time.

They arrived to find that the man was badly trapped, with one foot partially amputated. Hannah could see that they wouldn't be able to do much for him until the train was out of the way and she felt dread grip her.

She'd heard about this happening, but she'd never been present before when the potentially lethal manoeuvre was carried out.

'Has the electricity been switched off?' Leo demanded as he prepared to climb down onto the tracks. The last thing he needed to do was touch the live rail. . .

A railway employee confirmed that all the rails were safe, and Hannah watched Leo make his way along the side of the train until he reached the man trapped by the heavy steel.

She couldn't hear what he was saying, but she watched him trying to conduct some sort of examination between the wheels. Even in his protective clothing his arm looked so vulnerable against the sheer size of the machinery.

'Hannah, I need you down here,' he called, and she jumped in surprise. She'd honestly expected him to call for Nia's help.

With heart in her mouth, Hannah clambered down and made her way towards him.

'I'm going to have to go underneath with him,' Leo announced. 'I'll have to lie on top of him to hold him still while they drive the train off him. There isn't room to move and he's bleeding badly.'

Hannah had to clench her teeth to prevent herself from crying out against the idea of Leo putting himself in danger. All she could do was offer up a swift prayer for his safety and ask him what he wanted her to do.

It took a good five minutes for Leo to wriggle himself into position, and in the meantime Hannah had managed to set up an IV and had enlisted one of the station personnel to crouch on the platform above to hold the bag of fluid.

When the time came for the train to be moved it would have to be tucked underneath where the IV line couldn't be severed by the passage of the wheels, but at the moment at least it was doing something towards replacing the alarming amount of blood which seemed to be seeping out along the track.

'Hannah?' Leo's muffled voice called. 'I'm in position. Tell them it's safe to start moving the train—slowly!'

She relayed the message, but when Leo tried to get her to climb back up to the safety of the platform she refused.

'I've got to stay down here in case you need help,' she insisted. 'Everyone else will be too far away to hear, especially if the train is moving. Just tell me which rail to keep away from when they switch on and I'll be fine.'

He tried to argue but she wasn't listening.

'Switching power back on,' called the senior

railway employee, and Hannah repeated the message for Leo who flattened himself over the young man trapped beneath him.

Hannah's eyes were flicking continuously between the rails and the wheels, waiting to see the first sign of movement, so she nearly missed Leo's convulsive activity as his patient started to revive and began to fight his captivity.

Unfortunately his convulsive bid for freedom coincided with the first lurch as the train began to move, and Hannah was the only one to see the back of Leo's head struck by some unrecognisable lump of machinery.

Almost instantly he slumped bonelessly over the man beneath him, apparently unconscious.

'Stop!' Hannah shrieked as she saw his hand flop dangerously near the live rail. 'Switch the power off—quickly!'

There was a screech of brakes and the train came to a shuddering halt as her voice still echoed around the high ceiling of the station building.

'What's the matter?' John shouted as he tried to lean over far enough to see what had happened.

'The train hit Leo's head,' Hannah called

back as she scrambled between the carriages and lowered herself to the track. 'He's unconscious so I've got to protect him while they get the train out of the way.'

'Let me do it,' John insisted as he prepared to climb down.

'You can't—not enough room,' Hannah called back, not bothering to voice her determination that if anyone was going to take care of Leo it was going to be her. After the way she had hurt him it was the least she could do. . .

It was dark and cramped under the carriage and very cold, but none of that mattered when she ran her fingers through Leo's hair and felt the large lump coming up on the back of his head.

There was blood on her gloves when she drew her hand away so she knew the skin had been broken, and he wasn't responding to her voice.

Her heart thumped with fear as she slid carefully over the two men, grabbing hold of arms and checking that legs were out of harm's way as she spread herself over the top of Leo's inert form.

'Ready,' she called, careful to turn her head to the side as she tried to stay as low as possible.

With a groan and a clank the heavy vehicle started moving again.

John and Nia were waiting as daylight finally poured down on her, but when they would have helped her up she refused their assistance, concentrating on examining Leo's injury while they took care of their original patient.

'Leo,' she called softly as she ran her hands over his head again, fearful that she might have missed a more serious injury in her first assessment.

'Oh, my love, are you all right?' she murmured frantically. 'Oh, Leo, I love you. Speak to me...'

She crouched over him to shelter him from the chilly wind, hardly aware of the activity going on around her as a temporary tourniquet was applied to the suicide patient's leg before he was loaded swiftly onto a stretcher and lifted onto the platform.

She was hardly aware of what she was saying as she stroked Leo's thick hair away from his forehead in an agony of remorse. She could have lost him, without ever telling him that she loved him...

'Sister?' another voice intruded. 'If you'll give us a bit of space we'll get him out of there.

You can travel in the ambulance with him.'

She looked up into the familiar friendly face of Ted Larrabee and coloured when she realised how unprofessional she was being.

'Sorry, Ted,' she muttered, and felt the heat of embarrassment fill her face in spite of the bitter cold. 'I'll get out of your way.'

'Oh, no, you don't,' mumbled a familiar husky voice as Leo grabbed her hand and held it in place against his face. 'You're not going anywhere until you repeat what you said, but this time you're saying it in front of witnesses.'

'Leo. . . Are you all right?' she demanded as relief flooded through her.

'Not yet,' he mumbled as he rolled over to face her and trapped her other hand. 'But I will be as soon as you tell me what I want to hear. Tell me you love me. Tell me you can't resist me.'

'Oh, Leo, you idiot,' Hannah laughed through her tears.

'She must love you,' Ted butted in. 'It isn't every woman who'd climb under a train to take care of her man.' *Her man. . .*

Ted's words reminded her of the way she'd last seen Leo—laughing with Samantha and kissing her—and she remembered that Leo wasn't her man any more.

'No, Ted,' she corrected bravely. 'He's going out with Samantha from Obs and Gyn. . .'

'He certainly is not,' Leo objected, his eyes snapping fire. 'Whatever gave you that idea?'

'I saw you. . .this morning. . .' she began, then paused when she saw the glee in his face.

'You're jealous,' he whispered tauntingly as he pulled her towards himself. 'Jealous over nothing.'

'Nothing?' Hannah said, and bit her lip as hope began to blossom.

'She wanted to tell me that she's getting engaged—to that big good-looking physio that Tina's had her eye on. She apologised for chasing me and said it wasn't until she realised how I felt about you that she let herself notice the man who loved her.'

'Really?' Hannah squeaked, and felt a smile spread over her face.

'Really,' he confirmed. 'So now there's no reason why you shouldn't tell me what I want to hear.'

He sat there between the railway tracks with a boyishly expectant expression on his face.

'Oh, Leo, I *do* love you,' she said fervently, and framed his face in her hands for a kiss.

Time ceased to exist as their lips met, and it was only the sound of Ted insistently clearing his throat that brought the two of them back to their surroundings and the round of applause echoing across the platform.

'Your place or mine?' Leo offered huskily under the cover of the sound, his eyes darkened by desire to the colour of fine old brandy.

'Anywhere, so long as it's with you,' Hannah breathed and knew she meant every word.

'Leo?'

Hannah's voice was hesitant as she lay very still by his side, but she'd been lying here with her arms wrapped around him for a long time while she'd tried to compose her thoughts, and had finally found the courage to speak.

'Mmm?' The sound was a rumble in the depths of his chest under her ear, like the lazy purr of the lion he was named for, and for just a moment her arms tightened around him as she was overwhelmed by the realisation that today she'd come very close to losing him.

She'd sat beside him in the ambulance, perched on the edge of the trolley as they'd bumped and swayed towards St Augustine's, and when they'd reached the hospital he'd kept her by his side by the simple expedient of refusing to release her hand.

There had been an unmistakable gleam of approval in Wolff's eyes when he'd arrived to do the honours with Leo's scalp wound and had found the two of them together, Celia MacDonald's concern for an injured member of staff drawing her to prepare the suture tray herself.

'I expect superglue will be sufficient for the task, Sister,' he said with a grin as he drew her attention to their entwined hands. 'But I definitely think he'll need to take a couple of days off to recover from his injuries.'

Hannah looked up just in time to see the wink Wolff directed towards Big Mac.

'You think so, Doctor?' the senior sister said with an attempt at a frown that didn't manage to hide the twinkle in her eyes. 'In which case, do you think he ought to have someone with him to keep an eye on him? After all, he *has* suffered a head wound and he'll need someone to check up on him at intervals to make sure he isn't suffering from concussion. . .'

Hannah agreed to their suggestions with

alacrity, and drove Leo home with every intention of persuading him to sleep for a while, promising to wake him up at intervals to check that his reactions were still normal.

In the event, Leo had been the one to entice *her* into bed, seducing her shamelessly with words and caresses and the sort of kisses that made her forget her own name.

When he finally reached her last items of clothing she was unable to stop the reflex which brought her hands up to cover herself, but he was so gentle and matter-of-fact about her scars that she'd have dissolved into tears if he wasn't already arousing her beyond the point of embarrassment.

Their mutual pleasure in each other should have been proof enough that her disfigurement wasn't important to him but as she lay cradled in the warmth of his arms the doubts which she'd believed had been buried under an avalanche of ecstasy began to surface again and she knew she had to voice them.

'Leo, do. . .do you want me to have the implants done?'

Her stumbling question emerged in a rush, the words uncomfortable on her tongue, and when she felt the way silent tension suddenly filled his big body she almost wished she'd left well enough alone.

Had she spoiled everything by reminding him of all she could never be?

She'd once jokingly referred to the two of them as Beauty and the Beast and he'd pretended to bristle, not realising that she knew *he* was the beautiful one—her gorgeous tawny lion with the strangely compelling golden eyes—while she could never. . .

'No,' Leo said decisively, breaking into her fearful introspection with a jolt as he tightened his arm around her shoulders and tilted her face up so that she was forced to meet his eyes.

'I don't need you to have the implants done, Hannah, any more than I would want you to bleach your hair or wear coloured contact lenses—they wouldn't change the person you are inside. It's far more important to me to know that because of your bravery in having both breasts removed so quickly your cancer can't recur.'

'But?' she prompted when he paused. She'd heard the faint echo of pain in his voice and wondered if he was remembering when he'd lost Lisa. Her heart ached when she heard the unspoken reservation in his tone.

'But although you're still having check-ups you're passing with flying colours, and I think it would be a good idea for *your* sake if you had the implants done,' he continued softly, his sincerity clear in his eyes. 'I think it would give your self-confidence a boost—especially after the hatchet-job your ex-fiancé did on you.'

Hannah absorbed his words, revelling in the fact that his criteria were all based on her feelings until she remembered that some had wider implications. . .

'And. . .and what about children?' she questioned hesitantly. 'What if I can't—?'

'Lisa couldn't,' he reminded her bluntly. 'It didn't make a scrap of difference to me then, and it doesn't now. I love *you*, and whether we have children or not won't change that.'

Hannah gazed up into eyes that warmed her to her soul like clear golden sunlight and she thought for a moment. She sifted carefully through his words for the motives behind them and when she found only honesty and caring she was finally able to relax.

'Still. . .' he said, with a new huskiness creeping into his voice as his free hand slipped over the curve of her waist to caress her bottom and his fingers began a newly familiar path of exploration which took them closer and closer towards the liquid heat of her molten core.

'There's plenty of time to make decisions. . . There's no urgency about any of it,' he murmured distractedly as he teased her thighs into parting for him, his teeth closing gently on the softness of her lower lip before he soothed it with the tip of his tongue.

'No urgency?' she repeated as she felt the hard evidence of his own urgent desire against the curve of her hip and her breath caught in her throat.

'No urgency about anything except how soon you're going to marry me,' he muttered fiercely as he rolled over and pinned her underneath him in the middle of his enormous bed.

'And when you're going to stop talking and make love to me,' she murmured as she wrapped herself around him and welcomed him inside her body, revelling in the glorious completion.

She was still sprawled bonelessly across his body, her ragged breathing slowly returning to normal, when a stray memory floated to the surface to tease her.

'Leo. . .?' she began in a questioning tone, and he groaned dramatically as he flung his arms wide as if in abject surrender.

'Again. . .?' he exclaimed, as if in horror. 'Woman, you're going to kill me. . . Remember, I've been injured and I'm out of practice. . .'

Hannah chuckled at his nonsense.

'Not that I'm an expert, but it certainly doesn't show,' she commented cheekily as she ran teasing fingers over his broad muscled chest and followed the narrow curve of his waist towards his hip. 'I looked very carefully and I didn't see a sign of rust anywhere. . .'

He growled as he erupted and rolled her over to pin her beneath him again, his fingers tormenting her ribs mercilessly.

She shrieked with laughter as she retaliated, and they were both breathless when they finally declared a truce and retrieved the duvet from the floor at the foot of his enormous bed to wrap it cosily around them.

Hannah settled herself in his arms again, amazed that she felt as if she'd always belonged there—as if they'd been made especially for her—and suddenly she remembered what she'd wanted to ask.

'*Is* it just third time lucky for you, Leo?' she asked softly, her lips brushing against his neck as she voiced the tentative question. 'That's what the others were joking about when we went out for that meal with them. . .'

She felt his chuckle before she heard it, and her heart gave a silly leap when she heard the lazy indulgence in it.

'You can ask Polly and Laura about that, if you like, but you'll find that I've only ever been a friend to either of them,' he murmured, then paused long enough to hook one finger under her chin and raise her face for a tender kiss.

'I'd already met you,' he said quietly, his eyes intent as he scanned her face as if he wanted to be certain that she knew she had no need for jealousy. 'Met you, fallen in love with you and decided that I was going to wait for you to realise that you'd fallen in love with me too!'

'Such arrogance!' she exclaimed, laughing and loving him all the more for his patient constancy.

'But, then,' he added thoughtfully, 'I suppose some people could say that our love *is* third time lucky—after all, it'll be the third wedding in the A and E department in quick succession. . .'

Then, as she watched, his mouth curved in that familiar ladykiller grin, and her pulse leapt in response when she realised that she was going to be basking in that smile for the rest of her life.

'Ah, Hannah,' he murmured, his voice huskily intent. 'As far as I'm concerned, what we've found together is a once in a lifetime thing, and it's going to last a lifetime.'

'And beyond,' Hannah agreed as she gazed up into his loving eyes and her heart overflowed.

EPILOGUE

'TWINS!' Hannah squeaked in delight when her friend passed on the news. 'Oh, Laura. I couldn't be more delighted for you. When did you find out?'

'About an hour ago,' Laura said with a happy smile as she reached for her husband's hand. 'Wolff was with me for the ultrasound scan, and he'd just made some wisecrack about looking for a litter of Wolff cubs when the technician said there were two in the litter!'

'I bet that shocked you.' Hannah laughed as she looked up into his lean dark face.

'Not as much as when she pointed out the fact that they were conveniently positioned so that we could see what sex they were,' he said.

'And?' Hannah prompted eagerly. 'Did you opt to find out or are you waiting until they arrive?'

'We couldn't help seeing, whether we wanted to or not,' Laura said with a chuckle of her own. 'It's one of each.'

'Perfect,' Hannah said, and hugged her

friend over the pronounced bulge at her waist. She was already expanding visibly, even though she was barely four months pregnant.

'Especially if this is our only chance,' Laura said quietly. 'After all, I was told that the endometriosis could stop me having a family at all.'

'Well, all I can say is it couldn't have happened to a nicer couple. You and Wolff deserve them. . .both of them!'

'And the double lot of nappies and midnight feeds?' Leo queried as he joined them in the staff lounge, obviously overhearing enough of the conversation to realise what was going on. He kissed Laura's cheek and slapped his friend on the shoulder. 'Congratulations to both of you—enjoy the peace and quiet while you can.'

'You're here early,' Hannah said as she claimed a kiss of her own, her hand lingering lovingly on Leo's cheek. 'I thought you weren't due on duty for several hours yet. Did you come in for the results of the scan?'

'Not specifically,' Leo said with a grin. 'I had a phone call from Nick asking me to cover for him—Polly's been in labour for about twelve hours and they'd just taken her into the delivery suite.'

'He was cutting it a bit fine, wasn't he?'

Wolff commented, his dark brows meeting in a frown of concern. 'I'm surprised he didn't ask you to take over hours ago.'

'He would have done if he'd realised she was in labour. Polly only phoned him about an hour ago to tell him what was happening—said she didn't want him getting in a state when she wasn't sure if it was a false alarm.'

Hannah and Laura shared an understanding look.

Having lost one child, Nick had tended to treat Polly like a fragile flower while Polly's reaction to her own loss had been to make sure that she was kept as busy as possible. It was almost predictable that, without taking any silly risks, Polly would avoid going into hospital until the last moment.

'Anyway,' Leo continued, 'I phoned up a couple of minutes ago to find out how things were progressing. Apparently Nick arrived just in time to encourage her to push. Mother and daughter are doing well and father is delighted but still in shock.'

Amid exclamations of surprise and delight, there was one dissenting growl.

'If you try anything like that. . .' Wolff began, wagging a threatening finger at Laura.

'Don't worry, my love,' Laura said soothingly. 'By the time these two are ready to arrive I'll probably be only too pleased to put my feet up and let you do all the hard work. . .'

Leo wrapped his arms around Hannah's waist and she shivered deliciously as he tightened them until she was leaning against him, her head naturally falling back to rest on his shoulder.

'Shall we tell them?' Leo whispered in her ear, typically making the decision a joint one.

For just a second Hannah wanted to keep their secret to themselves for a little bit longer but then she nodded, turning her head to graze a kiss over his jaw.

'Actually,' he began, and had to pause to clear his throat. 'We've got a bit of news, too. Hannah's decided to postpone her surgery.'

There was a second's silence as Laura and Wolff took in the announcement, but they were obviously at a loss as to how they were supposed to react.

With Leo's encouragement, Hannah had finally told her friends about the traumas of the last couple of years, and had received nothing but support from them while she made her decision about having the implants done. For her to have changed her mind at such short notice was obviously puzzling them.

'What he hasn't told you,' Hannah added as she took pity on them, 'is that when I was having all my tests done before surgery they found out that I was pregnant so I decided—'

She didn't get a chance to finish before Laura and Wolff were swamping her with exclamations of pleasure and hugs of congratulations.

'So, what's it going to be?' Wolff asked when everything calmed down again. 'Are you going to go one better and manage triplets?'

'God, I hope not,' Leo said with a dramatic shudder, his arms tightening around Hannah again. 'It's enough of a shock to know there's *one* on the way.'

Hannah began to chuckle.

'I hate to think what the hospital grapevine is going to make of this when the news gets out—it was bad enough when one after the other of us paired up and got married, but now that we've all managed to get pregnant one after the other they're going to call us three of a kind!'

'I don't think that would be so bad,' Leo said, his voice slightly rough as he leaned his cheek against hers. 'All three couples have been lucky enough to find happiness within the last year so I say roll on the next year and here's to the future!'

'As long as it doesn't involve too many sets of twins,' Wolff added warily. 'We don't want an A and E department population explosion. . .'

MEDICAL ROMANCE™

Large Print

Titles for the next six months...

MEDICAL ROMANCE™

Large Print

November

December

January 1999